Angus is a Wakefield pack member, but Wakefield has never felt like home. Angus doesn't have a home.

Until he does.

Del has recently moved to Rosewood pack territory with his family, and he's a bit lost. His father has his younger sister, his brother has his mate, and Del feels out of place.

Then he meets Angus, and Angus tells him they're mates.

They're both hesitant in their relationship, and that's without the rest of their problems, like telling Angus's alpha that he's planning to move to Rosewood permanently and finding out who is auctioning rare shifters. Everything's a whirlwind, and Angus and Del will have to find their way to each other and their place in the world — and with the pack.

His Place in the World
Copyright © 2022 Catherine Lievens
ISBN: 978-1-4874-3704-6
Cover art by Angela Waters

Published by eXtasy Books Inc

Look for us online at:
www.eXtasybooks.com

# His Place in the World
## Legendary Shifters 9

### By

### Catherine Lievens

# CHAPTER ONE

There was a bounce to Angus's steps as he walked toward his office. How happy he was to be headed to the Rosewood pack made him feel guilty, but who could blame him? The Rosewood pack had been more welcoming than the Wakefield pack ever had, and there was no denying or ignoring that, even though the Wakefield pack had been his home for years. Or at least, that was how it was supposed to feel.

It didn't.

The building was silent, which he enjoyed. He'd arrived early on purpose, even though there was nothing he hated more than getting up at six in the morning. It was the only time he had some peace, though, and he wanted to take advantage of that. Unfortunately, his visit to the Rosewood pack wouldn't be long. He and Angela would probably be home tonight, and Angus already dreaded that.

He pushed open his office door as he sighed. He was thankful to Angela and the pack for welcoming him when he needed a home, but they'd never made him feel like he'd found one. Even after several years living with them, he was still an outsider, as several members never missed a chance to remind him. On the other hand, the Rosewood pack had always made Angus feel welcome, even though he didn't live with them.

Maybe it was because the Rosewood pack was made up of more than wolves. The same went for the Wakefield pack, but the shifters who weren't wolves were very few, including Angus. And while the others were normal shifters, he wasn't.

Why hadn't he chosen Rosewood when he'd been looking for help and a pack to belong to? Angus didn't have an answer. Maybe it was because Wakefield had been much bigger—and it still was. It had felt safer to have many shifters around him, and Angus had believed that in time, they'd feel like his family and that they'd protect him because they cared for him.

Instead, the Wakefield pack protected him only because he was a pack member. It was their duty, but that was where things ended. It was different in Rosewood, as Angus had seen. The shifters who lived with the Rosewood pack were a family, which was all Angus had ever wanted.

He flopped into his chair and sighed again. Thinking about it wouldn't help. If anything, it would make the situation more complicated, and that was the last thing anyone needed.

Angus grabbed his messenger bag from under the desk and started putting his things into it. The computer went first, along with the charger and the mouse. Then went a notebook, his favorite pen, and other bits and bobs. He wasted as much time as he could, but he was thankful that Angela had decided to set out for Rosewood early. She wanted to come back to Wakefield as soon as possible.

Angus wanted to never come back.

Once he was done packing his bag, he allowed himself a few moments to dream. What would happen if he asked the Rosewood pack alpha to become a Rosewood pack member? He didn't think Cam would have a problem with that, but what about Angela? Angus owed her a lot, possibly his life. She'd given him a safe place when he needed it, and she continued doing so. Angus had no doubt that if she knew how some Wakefield pack members treated him, she'd step in, but it wasn't because she cared about him. Angus wasn't sure she did. What she did care about was what he could do for the pack, and she wouldn't want to lose that. There was no way she'd agree to have Angus move, so it was probably pointless to dream about it.

But Angus couldn't stop himself from doing exactly that.

He shook his head at himself and his thoughts and grabbed his bag. Maybe Angela would already be awake. If she wasn't, he could shift and go for a run or maybe fly around for a bit. He didn't have many opportunities to do so, because someone might see him, but he always enjoyed it when he could.

Angus made sure everything in his office was locked tight, then left. Pack territory was still silent as he headed out, and he felt his body relax.

No one had ever been violent. They knew better, and Angela wouldn't hesitate to punish anyone who tried hurting Angus. He was an asset, and she couldn't afford for him to get hurt and put out of commission.

That didn't mean some pack members didn't hassle Angus. He'd never told Angela because he didn't want to sound like a whiny shifter who couldn't deal with people disliking him, but he was reaching the end of his patience.

He wasn't a wolf. So what? Why should that be a problem? The Rosewood pack made it work quite easily. They had many rare shifters, and all of them were happy. They'd found their mates with the Rosewood pack, and Angus knew that helped, but it wasn't like he could choose to find his mate. If he could, he wouldn't choose someone in the Wakefield pack.

Luckily for him, no one here was his mate. That meant that his mate was still somewhere out there, living his life while Angus yearned for him. Angus hoped he'd meet him one day, and that was one of the few things that pushed him to continue moving ahead. He needed to think about something good that would take him away from Wakefield.

He was just putting his bag into Angela's car when he heard footsteps behind him. His back went ramrod straight, and he sucked in a breath, hoping it wasn't someone here to bother him.

He should have known better.

"You think Angela's finally going to dump him some-where?" a male voice Angus knew well drawled.

"That would be good," another man answered.

Angus briefly closed his eyes, sucked in a breath, and opened them again. He wasn't a fighter, and he'd never been one. Most of his worth was proved on the computer, and these guys knew it. They weren't afraid of him or afraid to confront him. As long as Angela was nowhere to be seen, they were more than happy to poke and prod at Angus.

He turned to face them. Leonard's hair was all over the place as if he'd just rolled out of bed, which he probably had. Chances were it hadn't been *his* bed—not that Angus cared.

Angus crossed his arms over his chest. "What do you want?"

"Where are you going?" Mike asked.

"None of your business."

"We're pack members. What you do is our business."

They were pack members only when it was useful to them. Angus didn't say that out loud, though. It would only make them angry, and things never ended well for him when they were angry. "It's pack business. If you want to know where I'm going, you should ask Angela."

Mike snorted. "Why do you always hide behind her? Don't you have some pride? I asked *you* a question, not Angela."

"And if you want to know, you should ask her. I can't talk about pack business with anyone." Especially not about this meeting.

Leonard grunted. "We're not just anyone. We're pack members, more so than you. We deserve to know what's go-ing on."

"Until you're in charge, you don't deserve anything," An-gela's voice suddenly said.

Angus had to hide his smile as the alpha stepped out of her house. She was carrying a backpack and had her phone in her hand. She scowled at Leonard and Mike. Angus could have kissed her, but he knew better. She'd probably punch his lights out if he tried.

"Alpha," Mike said, lightly bowing his head.

Angela slammed her door shut and climbed down her porch steps. "What are the two of you doing here?"

"We wanted to see you off," Leonard said. "Neither of us likes the fact that you're going to Rosewood. Is it necessary?"

Angela's eyes narrowed. "Are you challenging my decisions as alpha?"

"Of course not."

"Then I don't see what the problem is."

"There are no problems, Alpha," Mike quickly said. "We're just worried."

"You shouldn't be. Angus and I will both be just fine. The Rosewood pack is an ally, and they won't do anything to hurt us."

"You can't know that for sure."

Angela opened the trunk of her car, dumped her backpack into it, and slammed it shut. "I don't care what the two of you think or believe. I know what I'm doing, while you don't. Stop sticking your noses where they don't belong." She turned to Angus. "Ready to go?"

Angus had never been more ready for anything. "Of course."

"Let's head out, then."

She climbed into her car, and Angus quickly followed. He wasn't afraid that Mike and Leonard would hurt him, but that didn't mean he wanted to spend more time than he strictly had to in their company. He was happy to leave them behind, and he slowly relaxed as Angela drove off.

"Everything okay?" she asked, startling him.

"Of course."

"Would you tell me if something wasn't?"

"You don't have to worry about me, Alpha. I'm fine and ready to work."

He could feel Angela's gaze on him, and he was grateful when she didn't add anything. He supposed that she didn't care how he felt as long as he was available to help the pack.

He wasn't one bit surprised.


Del landed on his back. The air slammed out of his lungs, and he stayed where he was, staring at the sky and the top of the trees. He should get back up and try to take down Kyle, but his entire body hurt.

Fighting wasn't for him.

Kyle's face appeared above Del. "Everything okay?" he asked, a worried frown twisting his expression. "Did I hurt you?"

Del shook his head. "Just my pride."

Kyle laughed. "Your pride is fine." He offered Del his hand. "Come on. I'll help you up."

Del didn't hesitate. He allowed Kyle to drag him to his feet. It seemed easy for Kyle, and it probably was. Kyle was a shifter, after all, while Del was human.

It was still hard to believe that now Del lived with a bunch of shifters. As he thought about that, he looked at his brother, Doyle. He was panting heavily, too, and he grinned at Del as if he was having fun.

He probably was. He wanted this. He wanted to become part of pack security, but Del, on the other hand, wanted nothing less. He was here to support his brother, but frankly, he was starting to rethink that.

"Are you done for today?" Kyle asked as he put his hands on his hips and looked at Del and Doyle.

"I am," Del quickly said. He didn't want Kyle to think he was willing to get beaten up again.

"I can train for a bit longer," Doyle said.

Kyle shook his head. "You don't have to prove anything, Doyle. I hope you know that."

"Of course."

But Del knew his brother. He could almost read Doyle's thoughts, and he was very much aware of the fact that Doyle felt like he *did* need to prove something. He had to prove to Kyle that he wasn't a bad person, even though he'd helped kidnap Kyle's mate. He wanted to prove to the Rosewood pack that they wouldn't regret giving him and his family a home and a place where they could live without worrying about where their next meal would come from. Del suspected Doyle was terrified that the Rosewood pack alpha would eventually kick them out. He couldn't say he wasn't worried about that, too, but he didn't actually think that would happen. The alpha was a good person.

He wouldn't have offered them a home if he wasn't.

Del flopped onto the forest floor and pressed his back against a tree. From here, he could watch his brother's ass get beaten by Kyle.

He couldn't help but wonder if Kyle enjoyed it. Even though Kyle and Doyle were friends, Del wondered if he had truly forgiven him for what he'd done.

Doyle wasn't a bad person. He'd been desperate for himself and their family, and he'd done something stupid. It could have ended badly for everyone involved, and it was still hard to believe that instead, Doyle and his entire family had moved in with the pack.

Doyle regretted what he'd done, and he was trying to prove it. He and Kyle had become friends, which made sense since Doyle was the mate of Kyle's best friend. Del wasn't sure he'd have been able to forgive Doyle if he'd been in

Kyle's place, but he wasn't, which was lucky for his brother.

Del stared at Doyle. He couldn't remember ever seeing his brother like this. Doyle had always been a nervous kind of person. He was jumpy, never seemed to stay still, and always looked vaguely afraid for his life. There were still remnants of that in his expression, but he was so much more relaxed that he almost seemed like a new person. Watching him duck Kyle's punches and laugh, Del couldn't help but smile.

Even though Doyle had made the biggest mistake of his life, things ended well, and that was all that mattered. Doyle and their family were safe, and they had nothing to worry about for the first time since Del could remember. He wouldn't change the situation for anything in the world, even though he felt like he didn't belong.

He supposed he didn't. He was human, and unlike Doyle, he hadn't found out he was a shifter's mate. Their father, Matt, hadn't, either, but things seemed easier for him, proba-bly because of Cora. Del's younger sister had taken to living with the pack as if she'd been born here, and everyone loved her. They seemed to like Del's father by association, and be-tween Matt's new job, the friends he was making through Cora, and everything else, he acted as if he'd always been a member of the Rosewood pack. Doyle did, too, although he was still hesitant in several ways.

Then, there was Del.

He was still signed up for college, but he was starting to wonder if that was what he wanted to do with his life. His father and even Doyle had sacrificed a lot to give him this op-portunity, and he didn't want to be ungrateful by squander-ing it, but his life had been turned upside down, and he didn't know how to deal with it. He felt like he was drifting and didn't belong, and while he wanted nothing more than for that to change, he didn't know how to make it happen.

But that didn't matter. None of it did. He'd be fine if his

family was safe and happy.

"I was wondering who was making so much noise in my backyard," a voice said, startling Del.

He looked up to find the alpha mate staring at Doyle and Kyle, who were now rolling on the ground. They were both in their human form, but Kyle was growling as if he was about to shift. Del had a moment of apprehension, but he reminded himself that no one here would hurt any member of his family, not even Kyle.

"Are we bothering you?" Kyle said as he got to his feet.

Toby smiled. "Not really, but I could use some help. Do the three of you want to help me set up things for the meeting?"

"What meeting?" Del asked as he got to his feet. He brushed his hands on his ass to get the dirt off.

"The Wakefield pack alpha is visiting with some of her people, along with the humans Everly found. They're going to try to help us with the auction thing."

Del shuffled his feet. He didn't feel like he fit in with the Rosewood pack, and he *knew* that was the case when they started talking about auctions and all that stuff.

He couldn't wrap his mind around the fact that some people captured, bought, and sold shifters as if they were nothing more than animals. Hell, even animals shouldn't be treated that way. Yet there were humans out there who abused shifters only because of what they were, and it was horrifying. The fact that Doyle had been involved in that, albeit briefly, didn't help.

"I'll help," Doyle quickly said.

Del almost rolled his eyes. His brother was too eager, and everyone knew why. "I'll help, too," he said.

Toby smiled and nodded. "Thank you. They should be arriving soon, and I want everything to be perfect."

"Even though they're coming for work?" Kyle asked.

"I don't know what to think of Angela," Toby admitted as

they started walking toward the house.

Del could see the house between the trees, and his heart accelerated. He might not be a shifter, but he was very aware of an alpha's role and how much power an alpha had. An alpha mate didn't have as much, but Toby was still second in pack hierarchy.

"The Wakefield pack is helping us," Doyle murmured.

"They are, but Angela doesn't strike me as a person who does things out of the goodness of her heart. I don't think she's a bad person, but she confuses me."

"And we have to work with them, because otherwise we'd be isolated and outnumbered," Kyle said.

"Exactly. She knows that, and she's taking advantage of it. I'm not saying Cam wouldn't, but I still don't like it. I also don't know what to think about the humans."

Del grunted. "Just because they're human doesn't mean they're going to hurt you," he pointed out.

Toby grinned at him. "I'm very much aware of that. I'm not wary of them because they're human. I'm wary because I don't know them."

"Which is why you're having this meeting," Kyle pointed out. "Come on. Show us what we need to do."

As it turned out, Toby needed help setting up chairs around Cam's office. He was in charge of the kitchen, getting refreshments ready. Del was glad Toby didn't need their help in the kitchen because he wouldn't have known where to start. He could boil water for instant ramen, but that was where his culinary ability ended.

"What do you think is going to happen during the meeting?" Doyle asked as they worked.

"I don't know." Whatever happened, though, it was none of Del's business. He had no intention of sticking around and finding out, even though Doyle was involved. He already had more than enough problems on his plate.

He didn't need to add more to it.

Angus was relieved when they finally reached the Rosewood pack. The tension in the car was made him afraid he'd say something stupid, and while he wasn't afraid of Angela, he wasn't comfortable with her.

He stumbled out of the car as soon as Angela stopped and took a deep breath, trying to free himself from the tension and everything that had been left unsaid between them.

"You don't have to make it seem like you're running away from me," Angela said. She slammed the driver's door closed.

"I'm not running away from you," Angus said.

"Could have fooled me." She looked around. Several cars were already parked in front of the alpha's house, which meant they were probably the last to arrive.

Angela disliked that, and she huffed in displeasure. "I should have kicked Leonard and Mike's ass. They made us late."

"I don't think Cam will mind."

"He won't. But that doesn't mean I want to make a bad impression on him and the humans."

Because that was who they were meeting with. Angus had looked into them after Cam had contacted Angela, but he hadn't been able to find anything nefarious. He'd dug pretty deep, but on the surface and even underneath, it seemed like they truly just wanted to help.

Angus hoped that would be true.

He grabbed his bag from the car, then followed Angela to the door. The porch steps creaked under their weight, and the door swung open before they could reach it.

"I thought I heard a car," Cam said.

The Rosewood pack alpha stood there, a smile on his face. He wore jeans and a t-shirt and gestured for Angus and

Angela to come into his house. "You're the last to arrive," he said.

Angela glared at him. "There's no need to point that out."

Cam wasn't one bit intimidated. Maybe it was because he was another alpha or because he didn't belong to the Wakefield pack. Either way, Angus admired that.

"Don't worry," Cam said. "No one's offended. Besides, Ryland only arrived a few minutes ago."

Angela's eyes narrowed. "How is he? Do you trust him?"

"I don't know yet. We haven't found anything that would lead us to believe he can't be trusted, but you know how these things go. You probably had Angus look into him, too."

Angela didn't confirm or deny, so neither did Angus. He didn't need to, anyway. They'd have been fools not to check out who Ryland was and why he had an interest in this situation.

Cam led the way toward his office. It wasn't the first time Angus had visited, although this definitely was the most serious time. They were finally getting somewhere with the auctions and finding rare shifters, which was their focus.

For Angus, it was a matter of life or death. He was a rare shifter himself, so he knew what it was like to be hunted and hurt because of that. He still wasn't quite sure what Angela's motives were, although he suspected that just like she had when she'd welcomed him into the Wakefield pack, she wanted rare shifters to move in so she could use them. She wanted the Wakefield pack to become bigger and stronger, so she needed more people. Wolf shifters would have been fine, but rare shifters would be better.

Angus swallowed. Angela always followed logic rather than her feelings, but that didn't mean she didn't like him. She'd always protected him and any other rare shifter who wanted to live with the Wakefield pack. Still, Angus couldn't imagine many would want that when the Rosewood pack was right there.

"Here they are," Cam declared as he walked into his office.

Angus followed, quickly looking around for an empty chair. A few people were still unfolding chairs so there would be enough for everyone.

One of them caught Angus's eye. He stared as the man unfolded one of the chairs he'd been carrying, set it against the wall, then set out a second chair.

The guy was cute. There was no denying that for anyone who had eyes. He was young, possibly in his early twenties, with dark hair and eyes. His focus kept jumping around the room, never stopping on anyone for more than a few seconds. The guy was nervous, and Angus could understand why. He wanted to tell him he shouldn't be, but that didn't feel like a good idea, considering he felt just as nervous as the guy looked.

"Thank you," Cam said to the guy as he and another guy who looked like him moved closer. "I'd like the two of you and Kyle to stay, since you're already here. You should eat with us once we're done talking, and besides, you're involved in this."

"We can just go home," the second guy said.

"Didn't I just tell you to stay?" Cam asked as he arched a brow.

The guy's cheeks flushed. "All right. Sorry, Alpha."

"Call me Cam. How many times will I have to tell you?"

"Sorry, Cam. We'll stick around."

Angus couldn't say he was sorry. He wanted to watch the other guy for a bit longer, but that wasn't why he was here. He and Angela had a job to do, and he was ready.

"Everyone, this is Angela, the Wakefield pack alpha," Cam declared, getting the attention of the people in the room. "The blond with her is Angus, a member of her pack."

Angus raised a hand and wiggled his fingers, then felt like

an idiot for doing so. Cam wasn't introducing him to his kindergarten class, for fuck's sake. With a huff, he flopped into one of the chairs and started taking out his computer.

"Angela, Angus, this is Ryland Young. As I already mentioned, he owns a private security company."

Angus peered at him, curious. He'd found out why Ryland was interested in helping them, so he trusted the guy as much as he could trust someone he didn't know.

Ryland Young had been in the military, and it showed. He still held himself as if he were a soldier, and he wasn't the only one. The guy with him behaved the same way.

"And this is Remington," Cam continued.

The guy with Ryland Young cleared his throat. "Remi, please."

"Of course." Cam looked around. "The other people here are Doyle, Del, and Kyle." Cam pointed at everyone as he introduced them, and Angus's heart accelerated when he learned that the name of the guy he'd noticed was Del.

"And this is Everly," Cam concluded, pointing at the man in question. "Is everyone ready to start?"

They sat on the chairs settled around the room. Angus felt he shouldn't be part of this meeting, and really, he was here only to help Angela. She wanted him to record everything and take notes, which he could easily do. He'd worked with Everly and knew his way around a computer, but nothing like the griffin shifter.

"Can you tell us more about your brother?" Cam asked Ryland.

Ryland and Remi exchanged a glance. They seemed to be close, and as he listened, Angus decided to look more into Remi. He wanted to know everything there was to know about everyone involved.

"We can go over it again," Ryland agreed. "Pembroke is my half-brother. We share a human father, but his mother is a shifter." He paused. "A rare shifter. I didn't realize it was odd until recently," Ryland said. "But then Pembroke was in my life for years. It was normal to me."

"He's not in your life now, though."

"He hasn't been for two years, since someone kidnapped him. I've been doing my best to find him, without success. We came close a few times, but every single one of those times, Pembroke disappeared again. I need to find my brother, and I don't care how it happens. I'm ready to deal with anyone who stands in my way, and I hope that's not a problem for you. You need help with these auctions and the people buying shifters, just like I need help finding Pembroke. That's why I believe we should work together. On our own, neither of us has had any results. Together, we could make a difference, and not just for Pembroke."

Angus leaned forward. He hoped Ryland was right. Pembroke and many other rare shifters needed help, and they could provide that help.

But only if they managed to work together.


Del had no place here, but since he was staying, he decided he'd make himself useful in any way possible. Right now, his only job was to listen to the information being shared, and he was more than happy to do that. He was having difficulty hiding the horror and disgust from his expression, though.

He wasn't surprised that human beings could be assholes. He'd had to deal with his fair share of those, and he'd have to do so again. He also suspected that, just like humans, some shifters were good people while others weren't.

But right now, in this situation, shifters weren't the ones behaving like monsters.

He already knew most of what was being said around him. He hadn't been involved in it, but Doyle was, and it was impossible not to be aware of it. Doyle had kidnapped Everly, a griffin shifter, because he'd been forced to. He'd needed the money for their family, and while Del was horrified by what Doyle had been ready to do, he understood where his brother had come from. He disagreed with Doyle's decision to kidnap Everly, but he'd already decided not to hold it against his brother, especially since, thanks to it all, their entire family was now safe.

Besides, Everly was fine. The pack had rescued him, and through the second man who'd kidnapped him, they were hoping they could find more about the auctions where Everly would have been sold.

That was what those people did. They found and captured rare shifters, then put them in an auction. Del could only imagine the kind of people who bought those shifters. He didn't want to get to know them or to find out why, and he didn't have to. The only people who would buy human beings, shifters or not, were monsters.

Del wanted to help, but he had no idea how. He was only human, and he hadn't been with the pack long. He wasn't sure there *was* anything he could do. He didn't understand why he was attending this meeting, but since he was, he decided to do everything he could to help. Maybe it would help him feel like he belonged.

For now, it didn't. It did make him feel like he had a purpose, though, which was something else he'd been looking for. Maybe this way, he'd be able to help the pack. That was all he wanted.

"What do you know about the auctions?" Cam asked.

Ryland looked pissed, although not at Cam's question. "Too much, yet at the same time, not enough. We've only been able to identify a few of the people involved. They were all small fishes, and none of them talked or gave us the names of the actual buyers and sellers. They know what they stand to lose, and they're not afraid of us. I think they believe that since we're human, we're not going to hurt them." Ryland swallowed so loudly that even Del could hear him from where he was. "Most of these people view shifters as little more than animals. That's why they have no problems with rich people buying and selling them. They treat them like animals, too. We've seen the places where some of the auctions are held. There was no one left behind, because rare shifters are too precious, but we saw the cages, and in some cases, the blood and everything else."

"But you don't agree that shifters are barely more than animals," Angela said.

Del didn't know what to think of her. She was an alpha, but she was nothing like Cam. She'd seemed pissed when she'd first walked in, and her expression hadn't changed. Hopefully, it just had to do with their situation, not with the people she was surrounded with. Del might not know her, but he could tell she wouldn't be easy to deal with if she got angry.

Ryland glared at her. "How can I think that when I raised my brother?"

"I don't know anything about you. How can I know what you feel about shifters?" Angela asked.

Ryland licked his lips. "I'm older than my brother by fifteen years. I was almost an adult when he was born, and unfortunately for him, neither of his parents were great. Our father was always more interested in his job than he was in his children, and Pembroke's mother preferred to travel than to spend time with him. I was the one who raised him, along with his nannies. He's the reason I decided to stay close by for college. I lived at home, and more often than not, it was just the two of us. I was there for him when he graduated from high school. I was there when he got his college degree." Ryland looked away. "But I wasn't there for him when he was kidnapped. He was twenty-three at the time, and that was two years ago. I haven't seen him since then, and it's like losing a limb. Some days, I can barely breathe through the pain."

Del's eyes burned. He felt sorry for Ryland, and if it was up to him, he'd agree to help right away. He wanted Ryland to get his brother back, and not just because of what might be happening to Pembroke.

There was no way to know what the people who bought rare shifters did with them. Del could only imagine it and disliked every option his brain gave him.

Cam cleared his throat. "We're sorry you and your brother had to go through that, but we'll find him."

Ryland cleared his throat. "Remi and I have been trying for the past two years, but we haven't been able to. With you, we will."

"We'll certainly do everything we can to make that happen. Now, tell us what you know about the auctions and the people involved. You got no details out of the people you found?"

"They're more afraid of their bosses than they are of us," Remi interjected. "They know we can't do anything to them. We're not involved with law enforcement, and so far, I managed to keep Ryland from doing something drastic. We might have to do just that if we don't make progress, though." He looked around. "We need to know whether or not that's something that will stop you from helping us."

Del couldn't be the one to answer that, and if he were in Cam's shoes, he'd be torn. He understood the need to do everything they could to find Pembroke and the other rare shifters being bought and sold, but he was pretty sure that Remi was talking about killing people. Could they really do something like that?

Thankfully, it wasn't his job, and it never would be. He was ready to help if Cam needed something, but not by killing anyone. He wouldn't be able to hurt a fly even if he tried, anyway.

"I can only talk for myself and my pack," Cam said. "But we've been in this fight for some time now. We'll do what we must to protect our pack and any rare shifter we find. I don't care if we're faced with other shifters or humans. No one deserves to be treated the way they're treating rare shifters."

Del had held his breath through Cam's speech, and now he released it. He wasn't surprised, and he couldn't say he disagreed with Cam's decision. He doubted there was any other way to solve the situation. These people, whoever they were, were rich and powerful. When it came to shifters, human law enforcement didn't seem to care much. They wouldn't step in and help, which meant Cam and the other shifters needed to do this on their own.

The thought of having people die over this made Del's stomach churn, but he could accept it.

Ryland nodded, clearly satisfied. "That's good to know."

"The same goes for the Wakefield pack," Angela added. "We'll help any shifter who needs us, and we won't hesitate to strike humans if we have to."

She sounded fierce, and while Del was glad that she was on their side, he couldn't help but wonder why she was doing it. Cam and his pack were involved because of Everly, but why was Angela?

Del wanted to believe she was doing this out of the goodness of her heart, but something told him that wasn't so.

# CHAPTER TWO

The meeting was over, and Angus should be headed home. He was happy to give Angela some time to chat with Cam, though. It gave him the opportunity to waste more time, which meant he'd get back to Wakefield late, which was what he wanted.

He shouldn't. Wakefield was his home, and by now, he should be used to it. He was, but that didn't change the fact that he dreaded going back.

He had a house in Wakefield. It wasn't big, but he was the only one who lived there. He was friendly with several people, but he didn't really have friends, and he certainly didn't have anyone he could have talked to about Mike and Leonard. They'd have told him that they were just joking around, but he was sure there was something else to their behavior.

They felt he didn't belong. Maybe it was because he wasn't a wolf shifter, or maybe because he was a rare shifter. Either way, they'd ensured he knew they didn't want him there, and he couldn't forget that. Even the people who were friendly with him didn't help, and every time he came to Rosewood, he couldn't help but imagine what his life would be if he lived here instead of in Wakefield. He was tempted to ask Angela to let him go, but she wouldn't. He wasn't a prisoner in Wakefield, but she knew what she had in her hands.

Angus wasn't just a rare shifter. He was also a hacker, and while he might not be the best, he wasn't bad at it. He'd helped protect the Wakefield pack in the past, and Angela wouldn't want to lose that, especially if he didn't have a good reason, and to her, a good reason wouldn't be *Leonard and Mike keep bothering me.*

So Angus was stuck, which was why he took advantage of what little time he still had in Rosewood.

The bottom of Angus's stomach dropped when he noticed Angela stepping away from Cam. He held his breath, hating himself for it. Wakefield wasn't that bad. He shouldn't be dreading going back the way he was.

Thankfully, Angela didn't come toward him. Instead, she moved toward Ryland, giving Angus a bit more respite.

Or at least, he thought so until he realized Cam was staring at him. He looked around, eager to find an escape, but the alpha was on him before he could.

"You're quiet today," Cam said.

Angus found himself smiling. "I didn't have anything to add. Everly's doing most of the work. I'm just here to support him."

"Still. I'd like to know what you think of the situation."

"What everyone thinks. It's horrible, and we need to step in. I'm glad you found Ryland, because it gives us an edge we didn't have before. Hopefully, between him and our packs, we'll manage to do some good."

"That's all I want. My people were lucky not to run into these auctions, although Everly was close. We know how much danger the rare shifters are in, and if I could, I'd save all of them."

Angus's gaze drifted to Angela. "You're not the only one." Although he still wasn't sure why Angela was helping rare shifters. Was it because she thought it was the right thing to do, or because she believed they could be useful to her? Maybe it was a mix of the two, and Angus couldn't blame her. She was an alpha, which meant her first focus was to keep her pack safe. If taking in more rare shifters helped with that, she'd do it without hesitating. She wouldn't force anyone to stay with them, but she'd find a way to make them want to stay.

The only problem was that it wasn't working for Angus anymore.

He was ready to move on. He was grateful to Angela for everything she'd done for him over the past few years. Without her and her pack, he might have been dead right now, or maybe auctioned off like so many rare shifters. Instead, he had his own home and a job, and he was safe.

But he wasn't happy.

Angela had given him what he needed back when he was alone, but he was ready for more. He wanted to find love, have a relationship, and build a life. He knew everyone in the Wakefield pack, and there was no one for him to share his life with there. He'd need to meet someone external to the pack, and while he hadn't met anyone in Rosewood, he felt like maybe here, he could. At the very least, he wanted to find out if that would be true, and there was no way for him to do that from Wakefield.

Besides, even if he didn't meet anyone in Rosewood, he felt more at home here than he ever had in Wakefield. Surely that should be reason enough for him to move on.

Shifters weren't obligated to stay with their birth pack or the pack they'd lived with the longest. They could move, and they didn't even have to find a new pack to do so. Shifters preferred to live in packs because it was safer, but Angus could leave Wakefield and drift around if he wanted to. Of course, for him, it would be more dangerous than it would be for a wolf shifter, for example. He could escape in a pinch if someone tried to catch him, but it would also be too easy for someone with bad intentions to capture him, and he'd never wanted to be in that situation.

Where did that leave him?

He hesitated. He'd never told Cam he was a rare shifter,

but maybe he should. At the very least, Cam should know who he was working with, right? It would help Cam feel like he could trust Angus even more than he already did, or at least, Angus hoped so.

He cleared his throat. "You created a safe place for rare shifters," he started, unsure how to bring it up.

"After meeting Sam and Toby, it was the least I could do," Cam said.

"You could have taken them in but refused everyone else. Rare shifters are safe here, but you're also putting your pack in danger by having so many of them living with you."

Cam frowned. "That's not going to stop me. No shifter deserves to be treated the way rare shifters are. They're exploited and sold off as if they're nothing more than objects, and I don't want that to happen to any of them. Besides, while having so many here puts my pack in danger, it gives them a home they're willing to fight for. They help keep the pack safe just like the pack keeps them safe."

Angus was making a mess out of this, and Cam was turning defensive. "I realize that. I wasn't trying to say anything negative. I just wanted you to know that as a rare shifter, I'm in awe of what you've created."

Cam's jaw dropped open. "You're a rare shifter?"

"I am. The Wakefield pack gave me home when I didn't have anyone else, and I'll always be grateful to them for that."

Cam cocked his head, still staring at Angus. Angus felt the alpha could read right through him, and maybe he could. From what Angus had seen, Cam was more in touch with his people than Angela ever had been.

She kept a certain distance between herself and her pack members. Angus wasn't sure she did it on purpose, but he felt like she believed she shouldn't be too familiar with them if she wanted to keep her authority. There was none of that here, though. Cam felt more like a friend than an alpha, although

Angus had seen him take control when he had to. He didn't know if that was the right way to behave, and frankly, he didn't care. He just knew he felt more at home here with Cam than he ever could in Wakefield.

Cam leaned closer, lowering his voice. "I'm glad you trusted me enough to tell me," he murmured.

Angus looked around, but Angela was still talking to Ryland and Remi. She didn't look happy, but then, she seldom did.

"And I want you to know that whatever happens, you'll always have a place here in Rosewood," Cam continued.

Angus blinked at him. "I'm sorry?"

"I want the Rosewood pack to be safe for everyone, not just rare shifters. They're not the only ones who live here, and I never intended for that to be the case. I'm open to new pack members, whoever they are and wherever they come from."

"I'm not sure what you're telling me."

"I'm just throwing it out there. Feel free to contact me if you need anything."

Angus was confused and felt like it would be better for him if he stepped away, so he nodded and did so. His heart raced. He wanted to believe what Cam was saying so badly.

Could he really have a home here in Rosewood? Could he take that step?

He was lost in his thoughts, so much that he didn't notice the man standing in the doorframe. He just needed out of this room and a breath of fresh air, and unfortunately, it meant that he slammed right against the guy standing at the door.

The man turned around and reached out to catch Angus before he could fall backward. The man—Del—frowned at Angus, who'd clearly interrupted his conversation with someone standing just outside the office.

He asked something, but Angus wasn't listening to him. He was staring because he couldn't look away, and it had nothing to do with the way Del looked this time.

When Angus had slammed against Del, he'd smelled him. Del wasn't just a cute guy Angus had noticed, and he never had been.

He was Angus's mate.


Del stared down at the cute guy, who didn't seem to have heard his question. "Are you okay?" he repeated.

Angus blinked. "What?"

Del frowned. Had Angus hit his head? That wasn't possible because Del would have seen it, but still. Something felt odd, and Del couldn't quite put his finger on what it was.

"I asked you if you were okay," Del said slowly. He hadn't heard Angus speak today, but maybe English wasn't his first language. Maybe he didn't understand what Del was saying.

Angus blinked again. "I'm fine," he croaked.

His English sounded flawless, so maybe he *was* from here. That meant Del still didn't have an explanation for how bewildered Angus appeared.

He dropped his hands now that he was sure Angus was steady on his feet. "Do you need to leave the office? I'm sorry I was blocking the way," he said as he stepped to the side.

But Angus didn't leave. Instead, he continued staring at Del until Del was uncomfortable. Something was happening, but what?

"Angus?" the Wakefield pack alpha asked, making both Del and Angus turn.

Angus's cheeks flushed. With his pale skin, it was very obvious, and Del found it endearing.

He'd noticed Angus right away in the office. How could he not have? Angus was adorable, and his blue eyes had pulled Del in. He had to be several years older than Del, but that wouldn't stop Del. Of course, the meeting wasn't the best situation to get to know someone, which was why he'd stayed away from Angus. He'd thought he'd have more time, but he'd been distracted by his brother, and now, it looked like Angus and his alpha were about to leave.

Angus turned his attention to her. "Yes?"

"We should head out. It'll take us a few hours to get home, and the meeting is over."

Del expected Angus to nod and go along, but instead, he stayed where he was. He looked around, seemingly searching for someone, although Del couldn't have said who.

"Everything okay?" Cam asked as he stepped in from the side.

Angus looked relieved to see him. "I was thinking about what you said to me earlier," he told Cam. "That offer is still open?"

Del felt he shouldn't be part of this conversation, but there was nowhere for him to go. He supposed he could step out of the office entirely, but Toby was behind him, listening in. He'd get everyone's attention if he tried leaving, which wasn't something he wanted to happen.

"What are you talking about?" Angela demanded to know.

Angus didn't even look at her. He was still staring at Cam, and his expression had turned slightly desperate. "I need to talk to you and Del," he said.

Del frowned. He didn't know Angus. Today was the first time they'd met, and he had no idea what the shifter would want to talk to him about.

"Angus?" Angela asked.

"To you, too, but to Del first. Please."

"We need to go home. We don't have a reason to stick around any longer," Angela said. Her voice was harsh, as if she suspected something was happening.

Del kind of wished she'd say what it was, because he was still confused as hell.

To his surprise, Angus grabbed his hand and pulled him to the side. Del didn't resist and was glad when Cam stepped in to stop Angela, who'd moved forward as if to stop Angus.

"Sorry about this," Angus murmured.

"You have nothing to be sorry about, although I have to admit I'm a bit confused. I feel like something's happening, but I have no idea what," Del told him.

They didn't go far, just outside the office. Doyle was still there, and he stared at Del until Del nodded. Then he winked and slipped into the office, leaving Del and Angus alone in the hallway. People were just a few steps away, and Del could hear their voices, but at the same time, being so close to Angus made him feel like they were the only people in the world.

Angus let go of Del's hand as if it had burned him and rubbed his palms on his thighs. He cleared his throat, swallowed, then cleared his throat again.

Why was he so nervous?

Del hoped he was about to get answers because he felt like he needed them soon. It was almost as if something was trying to jump out of his skin and reach for Angus, and he didn't have an explanation for that — or anything else happening.

"Are you a shifter?" Angus suddenly asked. "Because you don't smell like a shifter, and you'd already have reacted if you were one."

"I'm human," Del told him. "Can you please tell me what's going on?"

"You're my mate," Angus blurted out.

Del's brain froze. He felt like he couldn't make sense of the words, even though he understood them perfectly.

He was Angus's mate.

He'd seen Doyle with Marcus. He knew what being mates meant, and he'd even wondered if maybe a shifter out there would find him and tell him those words one day.

But not now. Not when he was only twenty and had just

moved in with the Rosewood pack.

Dozens of reasons why this was a bad idea crossed Del's mind. Dozens of reasons why this was the best thing in the world immediately followed. Del didn't know where to start, but maybe he should say something, because Angus looked spooked enough to start running if Del didn't.

Del opened his mouth, and while he had no idea what he was about to say, he didn't have to think about it because Angela burst out of the office.

"What's going on?" she asked.

Her voice sounded like she was ordering Angus to explain, and she probably was. This was confusing for Del, but it had to be even more confusing for the people watching them. After all, Angus had dragged him out of the office even though they didn't know each other.

Angus was still staring at Del. Del had no idea how to feel about his revelation, but he could tell he needed to tell Angus something. So, he did. "I honestly don't know how to feel about this, but I'm open to the possibility." This way, Angus would understand he'd need time to wrap his mind around the revelation but wasn't rejecting him right off.

Or at least, Del hoped so.

Angus's shoulders relaxed. "As long as you're not rejecting me, I can deal with anything," he murmured.

"Angus?" Cam asked. Unlike Angela, he sounded worried rather than angry. "Can you tell us what's going on?"

Angus straightened his shoulders and turned to face the alpha. "I apologize for my behavior, but I was overwhelmed when I bumped into Del and realized he's my mate."

Cam's frown turned into a wide smile, while Angela looked horrified.

"That's not possible," she said.

"Why not?" Angus asked. "I didn't make a mistake. I was close enough to him to smell him, and I'm sure he's my mate."

Angela's expression smoothed out. She seemed to have a lot of experience dealing with things she wasn't happy with and acting as if she didn't have feelings.

She stared at Del as if trying to read him. "Well, Angus is a member of the Wakefield pack. You're welcome to move in with us so the two of you can be together," she said.

Del's first instinct was to tell her *fuck no*, but he kept the words in. He didn't want to offend her, even though he didn't like her much.

"Or Angus could move in with the Rosewood pack," Cam said smoothly. "After all, Del just moved in with us, and this is where his entire family is. I'm sure you wouldn't ask him to move again so soon and to leave his family behind. Besides, he's going to college nearby. Rosewood is his home."

"Wakefield could become his home. If he's just moved here, he doesn't have a lot holding him back."

"As I explained, his entire family lives here."

Del was glad Cam had his back, because there was no way he was moving to Wakefield. He'd have said no even if he'd liked Angela, and that wasn't true, although he wasn't sure why. He just knew that his place was in Rosewood, and he wasn't going anywhere. What that meant for him and Angus, he didn't know, but he wouldn't change his mind.


Del hadn't rejected Angus. That was the only thing Angus could focus on until Angela asked Del to move in with the Wakefield pack. He'd half expected Del to say yes, and he could have kissed Cam when he'd intervened. Apparently, Cam wanted Del to stay in Rosewood, which meant he expected Angus to move there.

Angus was more than happy to do that.

But Angela *wasn't* happy. She was glaring at him as if he'd done this on purpose, and while he hadn't, he had to admit that he might have if he'd had the opportunity. As it was, he didn't have to come up with an excuse to move out of the Wakefield pack and in with the Rosewood pack. Del would be his excuse, or at least, he hoped so.

Angus had no idea what to think of any of this, and he could tell Del felt the same way. They were both confused, and with Del being human, things would be harder for him. Angus had always known that someday he might meet his mate. He'd been prepared for that to happen since he was a teenager. On the other hand, Del had probably imagined a future with a partner and children, all of them as human as he was.

And now, he'd been saddled with Angus.

Angus didn't even know if Del was attracted to guys, for fuck's sake. Yet even if Del wasn't, that wouldn't be enough for Angus to change his mind. Even if Del didn't want to be with him, Angus would use him as an excuse to move. They didn't have to be together if it wasn't something Del could deal with, although the thought broke Angus's heart.

But whatever happened between them, Angus's future was with the Rosewood pack. He was convinced of that.

He liked Angela, and he thought she liked him, too. She'd given him everything he could have hoped for when he'd needed it, but he'd never fooled himself into thinking she truly cared about him. His importance was in the skills he had as a hacker and what he could do for the pack, nothing more, nothing less. Here in Rosewood, he'd be cherished as a pack member, a friend, maybe even family. That was what he wanted — what he'd wanted all along.

"Angus's home is with the Wakefield pack," Angela said. "Where we should head back. I understand you're overwhelmed, Angus, but surely you need some time to wrap your mind around this? Wouldn't it be better for you to come home and give yourself some breathing room?"

Angus didn't want to make her angry. He didn't want her to hate him, and he suspected she knew he had no intention of ever living in Wakefield again. She sounded slightly desperate, although Angus was pretty sure he was the only one who could see that. He knew her much better than anyone else here.

Cam cleared his throat. "It's understandable that both Angus and Del need time to deal with the situation, but maybe they could both do it here."

Angela narrowed her eyes at him. "But Angus isn't your pack member."

"It doesn't mean I won't welcome him for as long as he needs. Clearly, one of them will have to move to be with the other if that's what they decide they want. I don't know Angus's situation with your pack, but I know Del, and I'm sure he'd be more comfortable here, surrounded by his family."

But Angus couldn't say the same because he didn't have a family. He didn't even have friends in Wakefield.

He needed to say something before Angela told Cam he was looking forward to going home to Wakefield. "There's no one waiting for me at home," he said. "I have no family in Wakefield, and I'll be more than happy to accept your offer and stay, at least until Del and I have talked and made decisions," he said quickly.

Angela looked like he'd betrayed her, and maybe he had. Maybe she felt like he was sleeping with the enemy, so to speak, even though both packs were allies.

But they hadn't been allies long. The Rosewood pack had always been much smaller, and Angela had never seen a need for them when it came to keeping her pack safe. Things were slowly changing, and Angela never did anything that didn't benefit the pack.

It had to be exhausting.

Losing Angus wouldn't benefit the Wakefield pack, but

Angus didn't care. It had never been home, just a place to stay, where people would keep him safe because they were supposed to. He wanted more than that. He wanted emotions and feelings, to make friends and have a family.

And all of that was within his reach.

Cam seemed delighted. "It's decided, then," he said, pointedly looking at Angela. "And, of course, it's not permanent. It won't be until they come to us and tell us what they've decided. I'll keep him safe, though. If that's what you were worried about, Angela, you shouldn't be. I realize my pack is much smaller than yours, but my pack members aren't any less fierce, and we've been doing a good job protecting our rare shifters. We'll do the same for Angus."

"You're a rare shifter?" Del asked.

There was so much they needed to talk about. Angus didn't even know where to start or if they should do it now. "I'm a Pegasus shifter," he told his mate.

Del frowned. "That's a horse, right?"

"With wings. Our cousins, unicorn shifters, are more famous, but we exist, too."

"Not being famous isn't a bad thing," Del murmured.

Angela suddenly grabbed Angus's arm. "I need to talk to you," she said. "If you'll excuse us," she told Cam and Del before dragging Angus down the hallway.

Angus's mouth went dry. He already knew what she wanted to tell him, but he wasn't going back to Wakefield, dammit. It might mean it didn't have a home, but he suspected that would change soon.

"What are you doing?" Angela asked, keeping her voice soft so Cam and Del wouldn't hear her.

"This is nothing against you," Angus told her.

"It sure feels like it is," she hissed. "What am I supposed to think of this? You didn't hesitate to accept Cam's offer to move out of the Wakefield pack and become a Rosewood pack member."

"That's not what he offered."

"But it is what will happen in the end, isn't it? You're not coming back to Wakefield, not permanently, anyway. Whatever you're saying, we both know that's the truth."

Angus had to look away. He'd never wanted to hurt her, but he needed to do what was best for him, not for her or the Wakefield pack. "I'll always be thankful to you and your pack for giving me a safe place to live," he said.

"But not so thankful that you'll stay with us and continue protecting us."

"You have many other people who can help you protect the pack. Besides, it's not like I did much. I just keep an eye on the security system and fix what needs to be fixed. You can find someone else to do that. You don't need me, and you never have."

"But you needed us."

Angus understood why she was angry and maybe desperate to keep him. She could find someone else to deal with the security system, but she'd have to train them. Before Angus had arrived, it had been much more rustic, and he'd implemented many changes because he'd needed to feel safe. It would be fairly easy to teach someone what to do, though. It wasn't what she wanted to hear, but it was the truth.

He breathed in and out for a few seconds, trying to stay calm. "I needed you, yes," he confirmed. "I was alone, and if you hadn't taken me in, I'd probably have been captured and auctioned like the people we're trying to rescue. I'll always be grateful for what you did for me, and I'll never forget it. I'm not saying I'll never come back, but you're right when you say I plan to move to Rosewood permanently if I can. It's nothing against you, Angela, but I've never felt fully at home with the Wakefield pack."

"And you feel at home here?"

Angus looked at Del, who was standing with Cam and staring back, looking worried. "Not yet, but I believe I could, in time." As long as Del gave him and their bond a chance, Angus knew Rosewood could become his home. Even if Del decided this was too much for him, Angus would be fine. He'd finally found a place where he belonged, something he'd been yearning for his entire life. He wouldn't let anyone take that away from him—not Angela, not Del.

No one.


Del couldn't look away from Angus. He wished he could hear what Angus and his alpha were whispering to each other, but he was only human and entirely too far away.

"How are you feeling?" Cam asked.

"Like I was hit by a truck."

"That's what meeting your mate will do. I remember when I first met Toby. I didn't expect it to happen, and I was stunned. Things went okay, though."

Del chuckled. "Considering the two of you are together and in love, I'd say they did."

"You and Angus can have that, too."

It was almost impossible for Del to imagine it. Before moving in with the pack, he'd never thought much about shifters. He hadn't had a reason to, and he'd needed to focus on college and helping his family. After his family had moved in with shifters, he couldn't avoid wondering about being a shifter's mate.

And now, he'd found out he was.

He cleared his throat. "Thanks for offering all of this to Angus," he said.

"Angus and I talked earlier, and I mentioned to him that he'd always be welcome here. I was surprised to find out he's a rare shifter, but even if he hadn't been, I would have offered the same."

"Why?"

"Because I don't think he's happy in Wakefield. Knowing he's a rare shifter makes that more understandable, especially with what I know about the Wakefield pack."

Del frowned. "Are they not a good pack?"

"That's not what I said. Angela is a good alpha and does everything she can to keep her pack safe. There are many more Wakefield pack members than there are Rosewood, so her job is harder than mine."

Del glanced at her. He still wasn't sure what to think of her, but her behavior and Cam's were incredibly different. She was much more rigid, and there was no friendship between her and Angus, although maybe that was because of the situation. To Del, though, it felt like her relationship with Angus was much more professional, while Cam's relationship with every single pack member was that of a friend. Everyone knew he was in charge, but he didn't need to order people around or raise his voice for them to do what he asked.

"You expect Angus to want to become a Rosewood pack member eventually," Del said.

"I do, and I expected it even before he realized you're his mate. I've only met him a few times, but he never seemed happy. I understood what was happening when he mentioned the pack and how I made it a safe place for everyone. If he wants to live with us, I'm more than okay with it. The fact that you're his mate will make things easier for him when it comes to the Wakefield pack. Angela will probably still try to stop him, but doing so would mean keeping the two of you apart."

And from what Del understood, that was something most shifters wouldn't do.

They viewed mates as a sign of fate and didn't separate them. Del was sure that some shifters didn't care about mates,

35

especially when it came to other people's mates, but that wasn't a problem in the Rosewood pack.

Cam would give Del and Angus the time and space they needed to figure things out. He wouldn't force them to stay apart or to be together. That was all Del could have hoped for, along with Angus moving in with the Rosewood pack, which was apparently happening.

Cam cleared his throat. "Angela, why don't you come with me back to my office? We can talk about how we'll organize this. I'm sure Angus wants more time with Del, so maybe he could stay here right away, and you could send someone back with his things? Or I can send someone with you to pack what he needs and bring it back."

"I don't need anything I can't buy here in town," Angus quickly said. It was almost as if he was afraid Angela would find a reason for him to go back and stay. "I'll be fine for a couple of days."

"You might need more than a couple of days to decide what you want to do," Cam pointed out.

He moved toward Angus and Angela, and Del quickly went with him. He didn't want to leave Angus alone with Angela.

"We'll see what happens in a few days, then." Angus's smile was tense. "But I'll be fine with a pair of jeans and a few t-shirts. I'm not here on vacation, after all. I'm here to talk things out with Del and continue working on the auctions and our plan. I can do that from here as well as I can from Wakefield, since I have my computer with me." He looked at Angela. "I can also keep an eye on the security system and even train someone else from here. You'll have to choose that person, but once you do, have them contact me."

Angela opened her mouth, no doubt to protest, but Cam hooked his arm around hers and pulled her back toward his office. "See? He's already thought of everything. The

Wakefield pack will be fine, at least for a few days. Once they decide what they want to do, we can fix the rest."

Del had no doubt Cam was leaving him and Angus alone on purpose. He was nervous, but he needed answers, and he was glad to have the opportunity to get them.

"It seemed like me being your mate is complicating your life," he murmured, looking at Angus.

Angus beamed at him. "Are you kidding me? You being my mate is everything I could have hoped for."

Angus's answer startled a chuckle out of Del. "But you don't know me. Maybe I'll leave the toothpaste open on the sink the entire night. Maybe I don't put my dirty socks in the wash." Del did all those things, and he was pretty sure Angus would find them annoying.

To Del's surprise, Angus leaned closer and kissed his cheek. "I have no doubt we can drive each other nuts and that we will eventually. But I was thinking about a way to move out of the Wakefield pack and possibly in with the Rosewood pack, and you dropped in my lap. It doesn't matter how nuts you drive me. I'll always be grateful for that."

"Why did you want to move away from Wakefield?" Del was terrified that someone was hurting Angus, even though they'd just met each other. He shouldn't care about this man as much as he did already, but knowing what he did about mates, he understood why he felt that way.

Angus shrugged. "It's never been a home. Angela took me in, and I'll always be grateful for that, but I want more in my life than just surviving and helping the Wakefield pack. I want a real home, friends, and a family eventually. That never happened in the years I was with the Wakefield pack, but maybe it will now."

The thought of having a family with Angus made Del panic, but he could tell Angus wasn't saying they needed to do it now. He was slightly older, so maybe he was more ready than Del to start a family, but Del suspected he wouldn't push. That didn't seem to be the kind of person Angus was, and besides, they had many things to sort out before they could talk about children or whatever having a family meant to Angus.

Del cleared his throat and offered Angus his hand. "I guess I should introduce myself. My name is Del, and I'm twenty. As I told you before, I'm human, and I just moved in with the Rosewood pack because my brother found his mate here." Del felt slightly stupid introducing himself like this, but Angus appeared delighted and shook his hand.

"I'm Angus, and I'm twenty-six. I'm a Pegasus shifter, one of the rare shifters I'm sure you've heard about. I've been with the Wakefield pack for close to five years now, and it's time for me to move on, hopefully with you."

Del's mouth was dry. "Maybe. I'm going to need time, though. Moving in with shifters was confusing enough, and I'll admit I have no idea what to do with you."

Angus was still holding Del's hand, and he squeezed Del's fingers. "That's perfectly fine with me. I don't expect you to know what you want right away. I don't even know what *I* want. We'll take things slow and see where they lead us."

That was all Del could have hoped for, and he was glad Angus was giving it to him. Knowing he had a mate was confusing, but Del didn't have to deal with the knowledge on his own. He could talk to his father, to Doyle, who would understand it better, and of course, to Angus. They'd find a way to make it work.

And didn't that mean that Del was ready to give Angus a chance already?

# CHAPTER THREE

"Good morning."

Angus looked up from his computer screen, blinking at Toby. It took him a second to understand what the alpha mate had said, and when he did, he grinned. Toby didn't seem offended that he hadn't said *good morning* back yet. If anything, he appeared amused as he sipped from his cup of coffee while leaning against the kitchen counter.

"Good morning," Angus said.

Toby smiled over his cup of coffee. "I wasn't sure you'd heard me. I've been in the kitchen for several minutes, and you haven't noticed. I even got myself coffee."

"Sorry about that. I was in the middle of something."

"You're always in the middle of something."

That much was true. Angus had moved in with Cam and Toby and was currently living in one of their guestrooms. When he'd decided to stay with the Rosewood pack for a while to get to know his mate, he hadn't been sure where he would be staying. He didn't think staying with Del was a good idea, especially after discovering Del lived with his father and his younger sister. He wanted to get to know his mate, but immediately sharing a home with him hadn't felt like the best idea. They'd do so eventually, but it was way too soon, especially since Angus wasn't used to living with the Rosewood pack.

Thankfully, Cam had thought of everything. As soon as Angela had agreed that Angus could stay, he'd offered one of his guestrooms, pointing out that this was why he had them and that Angus would be able to come and go as he pleased as long as he didn't bother him and Toby too much.

Angus had no intention of bothering them. Between Del and his job, he had more than enough things keeping him busy. He'd barely even seen Cam and Toby since he'd moved in with them, and he'd been here several days.

Toby pushed away from the counter and came to stand behind Angus. He leaned forward and peered at the screen, and Angus let him. Toby might as well be an extension of Cam. He knew everything there was to know about what they were working on, and, like Angus, he was a rare shifter. He'd been taken from his home when he was young, kept as a healer by a gang, and had only been rescued after the Rosewood pack had found his brother. Angus had heard all about Toby's story during his first dinner with him and Cam, and he was still in awe.

Most rare shifters shared stories of pain and fear. Toby's story wasn't any different, and it made Angus feel close to him. Maybe he shouldn't feel like that, but to him, it was one more reason he should move in with the Rosewood pack permanently.

But that wasn't something he could afford to think about right now.

Angus already knew it was what he wanted. Things with Del still felt awkward and unsteady, but that was only because they barely knew each other. One of the conditions Angela had given Angus to stay with the Rosewood pack was that he wouldn't stop working, and he didn't want her to call him home, so that was what he'd been doing. He was with Del every second Del wasn't involved with college or his family. The rest of the time, Angus was on his computer, trying to find out more about the auctions.

Unfortunately for him and all the rare shifters involved, the man who'd tried to sell Everly to the auctioneers wasn't talking. Doyle, Del's brother, didn't know anything more than what he'd already shared, even though Angus had tried talking to him a few times. He was pretty sure Doyle had only given him the time of day because he was Del's mate. Angus had been surprised to find out Del had told him and suspected it was because he'd wanted to know what his brother thought of it. Doyle was a human and a shifter's mate, so he'd know better than most what Del was going through.

"What are all these names?" Toby asked.

"Everly gave me access to his rare shifters forum. I've been tracking rare shifters, especially the ones who seemingly disappeared without leaving a trace."

"You think they were found by these people and auctioned off?"

"Probably not all of them." After all, rare shifters died, too.

For most of them, it wasn't from old age, unfortunately. Accidents happened, though, and Angus had even found a few vanished shifters who'd disappeared from the forum because they'd found a safe place to stay and had built a life there. Those people were always more than happy to tell Angus about their new life. Most had promised they'd contact him if they learned anything about the auctions.

So far, none of them had.

As frustrating as it was, Angus was glad for that. Those shifters were out. They were living their life, finally unafraid of being hurt, and he didn't want to ruin that for them. He couldn't bring unwanted attention to them through his research, so as soon as he was sure they were okay, he deleted their names. Hopefully, the people involved with the auctions wouldn't find the forum. As far as Angus knew, they weren't aware of it, and even if they were, Everly was too good with security and computers to allow them in. The forum was hackproof, and it would stay that way.

"There are so many names," Toby whispered.

There were. Angus had been surprised at how many rare shifters were registered on the forum. Everly tried to keep things as anonymous as possible, but he couldn't allow just anyone on the forum. It wouldn't be unheard of for someone to try to use it to find rare shifters. There had been several hacking attempts, but Everly seemed to find them amusing rather than worrying.

"There are more rare shifters in the country than I expected," Angus agreed.

"And how many of these people are missing?"

"Too many of them. The problem is that it's almost impossible to find them once they're gone from the forum. Everly keeps it anonymous for a reason, and even with my computer skills and the little info he has, it's not easy."

"What have you been doing, then?"

"Well, the first thing I do is take these names and google them."

Toby snorted. "That's it?"

"It's a good start. I find everything I can on these people, and then I start digging."

He copied and pasted one of the names on the list to show Toby. The google search didn't seem that interesting at first glance, but Angus narrowed his eyes at the sight of a name several search results down.

He'd seen that name before.

He looked down at his notebook, trying to locate it. It took him a moment, but his heart skipped a beat when he did.

He quickly opened a new window, then searched the name, first on its own, then along with some of the names of the shifters he was looking for.

He didn't get hits for all of it, but he got enough of them to know it wasn't a coincidence.

"Who's Albert McGrath?" Toby asked.

"I don't know yet," Angus murmured. "I need more time.

He's connected to several of the shifters who disappeared."

Finding Albert was easy. He was on all the social media, usually posing with men who looked like him. Angus got an explanation for that when he found out that Albert was the co-owner of a security company.

"How is he connected to the shifters?"

Angus was only half listening to Toby but telling him what he was finding as he worked helped him gather his thoughts. "On the surface, in no way at all. A few of the vanished shifters have mentioned him in the forum or on social media, though." Angus searched the forum for Albert's name. "A few times, they asked if anyone had heard about Albert. Other times, they say Albert offered to help them."

"But you don't think he actually helps them."

"I don't know."

Angus dug deeper into Albert's life. Albert's security company had many clients. Angus would have to research all of them, but he didn't have to go far to know he'd found something.

One of Albert's clients had apparently hired the security company for several parties. That made sense, and there was nothing strange about it, or at least, there wouldn't be if Angus didn't suspect Albert was involved in the vanishing of rare shifters.

"Albert works for many influential and rich people," he explained. "He provides security for events, from weddings to funerals to parties."

"What kind of parties?"

Toby's question was smart.

"I don't know yet, but I'll find out." It was a promise Angus had every intention of keeping.

He only had his instinct to go on, but he was sure he'd found something important. Whether or not it would help them, he wouldn't know until he was further in his research, but he'd dig up everything he could on Albert, including his favorite brand of underwear and his grandmother's maiden name.

If Albert was involved in the auctions, Angus *would* find out.

Del was walking around in the forest, taking a break from studying, when he heard the sound of vehicles. That was strange because most people moved on foot in pack territory, so he decided to take a look. He wouldn't be able to do anything if the pack was being attacked, but that was probably not the case.

Or at least, he hoped not.

He followed the sounds toward Cam's house. It was at the center of pack territory, with others sprinkled around it. They all faced the central bonfire Del had seen used several times already. He'd even spent time sitting there next to the fire, getting to know Angus.

And he had no doubt Angus was involved in whatever was happening.

The cars had parked by Cam's house, and Del recognized the man climbing out of one of them. Ryland wasn't wearing a suit today. He looked like he'd been training when someone told him to come, and he was still wearing shorts and a t-shirt. His cheeks were flushed, and if Del hadn't already been falling for Angus, he might have given Ryland a thought. His father wouldn't have been happy about that because Ryland had to be twice Del's age, but Del had never cared about age.

Still, he was glad Angus was still in his mid-twenties. That made it easier for them to get along and understand each other.

Remi got out of the other car, and he and Ryland walked toward each other. Their presence here, clearly unplanned, was enough to tell Del that something had happened. He wasn't fully involved in any of this, but between what Doyle had done, Everly being a rare shifter, and Angus, he felt he had a right to know what was going on. So instead of heading home, he headed toward Cam's house.

He got there as Ryland and Remi climbed the porch steps. The two of them heard him and turned to face him, and while Remi frowned, Ryland smiled at him and offered him his hand.

"Del, right?" he asked.

Del shook his hand and nodded. "You got it right."

"It's good to see you again. Are you here for this impromptu meeting?"

"Not exactly, but I'd like to know what's going on, considering my mate is involved."

"Really? I wasn't aware of that."

Del shrugged as he followed Ryland and Remi toward the front door. "We only recently met, but he was there during the last meeting."

"The cute blond?"

Del narrowed his eyes at Ryland, who laughed.

"Sorry about that," Ryland said. "But your mate *is* cute."

Angus was, and Del wasn't actually angry. Ryland had eyes, and as long as he didn't bother Angus, Del didn't care what he thought of him.

Ryland knocked on the door. It took a few moments for someone to open. Toby didn't seem surprised to see them, although he did arch a brow at Del, who looked away, hoping the alpha mate wouldn't ask him to leave.

"We came as quickly as we could," Ryland said. He and Remi walked in, and Del quickly followed.

"We were sorry to bother you today, but we need to talk to you," Toby said. "Or at least Cam does. He's in his office with Angus. You can head right there."

"Have you found Pembroke?"

Toby grimaced. "Not as far as we know, sorry. We might be a step closer to finding him, though."

Apparently, that was all Ryland needed to hear. He rushed down the hallway, heading toward the office. Remi went after him, but when Del moved to follow, Toby grabbed his arm.

"You realize you don't have to be involved in this, right?" he asked.

"I don't especially want to, but I also can't look away and ignore the situation," Del told him. "Between Doyle and Angus, I need to know what's going on. If there's anything I can do to help, I will."

Although Del doubted there was much he could do. Ryland and Remi were human, too, but they were older, had great jobs, and a lot of money. Del couldn't compare to that, and honestly, he didn't want to. He just wanted to be there in case anything happened.

Toby nodded. Del didn't wait for Toby to change his mind. He rushed toward the office, walking in as Angus spoke.

"Through this Albert guy, I managed to find several of his clients, including one who organized a party for this weekend," he explained.

"What kind of party?" Ryland asked.

He and Remi sat in front of Cam's desk, where Angus was. Cam was on his side of the desk, and while he looked surprised to see Del here, he didn't tell him to leave. Del closed the door before taking the last empty chair on Angus's other side.

Angus didn't even look up from his computer. Del wasn't offended because he'd already seen his mate while he was working, and he knew this was normal. Angus was fully focused on what he was doing, and Del wouldn't want him any other way.

He loved watching Angus work. When Angus was focused

on his job, he was in his own world, and that allowed Del to watch him without him knowing. Angus was passionate about finding these shifters, and Del didn't blame him. He wanted to find them, too, although considering he was only human, it made sense that he wasn't as focused.

"Well, the invitation doesn't specify it's an auction, but I believe it is," Angus said.

"Why?" Remi asked.

"Because of the wording and the people invited. Not only are they the richest people this guy knows, but the invitation is weird. It says they're invited for a night of drinks, fun, good food, and choices. It also says that the people invited shouldn't mention it to anyone else."

"How did you get your hand on an invitation?"

"I hacked into someone's account. He's one of the co-owners of the security company working the event. I have the list of the people invited, and if we need to, I can create another invitation." Angus looked up, his gaze stopping on Del. He blinked as if he wasn't quite sure what to make of Del's presence, so Del smiled at him.

He didn't need Angus to focus on him. He just wanted to be here for his mate, and he was.

"Why would we want to create another invitation?" Cam asked.

"Because having one would mean we could get into the auction," Angus explained. "Think about it. So far, we don't have anything concrete. I can think whatever I want, but I can't make any promises until I have proof that this is an auction. I believe we should get someone in, but we need funds. We could fake it, but I think it would be better if we had someone backing us who has access to a lot of money."

"Which is where I come in," Ryland added.

Angus nodded. "I can hack into the system and fabricate this invitation, but if we're doing this, we need to play it well.

Are you a good actor?"

"I can be if it means I might get my brother back."

"Then I believe you should go to this party, and since the invitation also states that pets are welcome, you should take me with you."

Del's stomach turned to lead. What was Angus talking about?

"You're not a pet," Ryland pointed out.

"But they're not talking about animals here. Come on, Ryland. Can't you see it? If this truly is an auction, and I believe it is, the people invited are used to buying and selling shifters. Why do they do it? I'm sure all of them have their own reason, and one of those reasons is that they enjoy having rare shifters as pets. I could take advantage of the situation to clone cell phones and maybe even sneak around and get more information."

"What if someone realizes Ryland wasn't supposed to be invited?" Remi asked.

"Why would they? Even if no one recognizes him, he can say he's a friend of a friend of the organizer. Anyone looking into him will find what I want them to find, including Ryland's bank accounts. Besides, since he owns a security company, he could be looking both for pets and fighters. He's not the only security company involved, after all. Having me with you would help our cause and show everyone that you're serious about the auction and that you're actually contemplating buying more shifters."

Del understood everything Angus was saying, but his brain couldn't make sense of it. Was Angus actually willing to put himself in danger that way? It sounded like he was, and Del wasn't sure what he could do about it.

Or even if there *was* anything he could do about it.

"What if this is an auction?" Cam asked. "Will you just be gathering information, or are you planning on trying to save the shifters there?"

Angus hadn't gotten that far. "My first instinct would be to save everyone we see, but I don't think that will be possible."

"I agree," Remi said. He glared at Ryland when Ryland opened his mouth. "And I know that if Pembroke is there, all hell will break loose. I don't expect you not to do anything if you find your brother. But think about it. What will happen if you decide to step in and attempt to save all the shifters these people are auctioning? You can't buy all of them, and if you try, people will notice and know something's wrong. What will happen to you then? What will happen to Angus or any of the shifters involved?"

Ryland's heart looked like it was breaking, and Angus understood. He wanted to save rare shifters, too.

But they wouldn't be able to, at least not the night of the party.

"We'll gather as much information as possible while we're there," he said. "Hopefully, that will include information about where the rare shifters are being kept between auctions. If we can find an address, these shifters will be easier to rescue than the ones who get sold. We'll get all of them eventually, though." It was a promise that Angus was making to Ryland and the others as much as he was making it to himself.

"And you're willing to put yourself in danger for this information," Del said.

He was staring at Angus, but Angus couldn't read his expression. It was fairly easy to understand how he felt, though. Angus just had to think about how he'd feel if Del volunteered for a mission like the one he'd just volunteered for.

His mouth went dry. He understood where Del was coming from, but that didn't mean his mate's feelings would stop him. This was too important, maybe even more important than a mate. "This is the best way to get me inside and for me to find the information we need," he explained.

"You could get hurt."

"I could get hurt here without even walking out the door. I could get hurt on my way back to Wakefield. I was lucky enough to find not one but two places to call home. I was able to get off the street and be safe. I want every single rare shifter to have the same and for all of them to be free to make their own decisions. These people, the whole operation, needs to be shut down. If the only way to get the information I'll need to make that happen is to go there and act as if I'm Ryland's pet, I'll do it."

Angus wasn't used to having to keep in mind other people's feelings when he made decisions. He was careful of Angela, but usually, she went along with whatever he said. She knew he wouldn't do anything without a good reason, and he had no doubt she'd agree.

"I'm not letting you go on this mission on your own. If you're going, then I am, too," Del said.

Angus was annoyed. Didn't Del realize he could take care of himself? He'd been doing so since he was a teenager, and while he was safer now than he'd been with the Wakefield pack, he'd always be careful of his surroundings and the people around him. He'd made sure he could defend himself if someone tried attacking him, and he knew what he'd be walking in to if he went on this mission.

"You can't go," he declared.

"Why not? Because I'm human?"

"Exactly."

"Ryland is human," Del pointed out, looking smug.

"And I wouldn't be asking him to do this if I didn't need him to."

The sound of something crashing in the hallway made all of them jump and turn toward the door. Angus heard someone talking, but no one came in, so he turned back to the problem at hand. "We need to put as few people as possible in danger. Ryland needs to go, as do I, because beyond Everly, I'm the only one who can gather this information, and considering he was kidnapped once, we can't put him in the spotlight that way."

Del crossed his arms over his chest. "Do you think the other people invited to the auction will have bodyguards?"

Angus frowned. "Probably. Why?"

"Ryland will need bodyguards, too. It wouldn't look good if he didn't, right?"

Angus's stomach churned. He knew where Del was going. "You can't be his bodyguard."

"So you're telling me that I can't forbid you to go on this mission, but you can tell me to stay back?"

The door opened suddenly, slamming against the wall and revealing a man holding a little girl. She clung to his neck, hiding her face against it.

Angus hadn't officially met Matt, but he knew who the man was, and having him there, glaring at Del, couldn't be good.

"Are you out of your mind?" Matt asked, stomping inside the room and stopping in front of his son. "How can you think they'll allow you to go?"

Del threw his hands in the air. "Have you and Angus agreed on this? I'm an adult. Neither of you can forbid me to do anything."

"I might not be able to, but Cam is your alpha, and I'm sure he sees how stupid sending you there would be."

They turned as one toward the alpha. Angus was glad he wasn't in Cam's place because he wasn't sure what he would have done if he had been.

"If the other people present at the auction have bodyguards, it makes sense for Ryland to have them, too," Cam said slowly.

"I'll be one of those bodyguards," Remi said with a grunt.

"As will I," Del said.

"My answer to both those suggestions is no," Ryland stepped in. He raised a hand, stopping both Remi and Del before they could argue. "Think about it. What if something happens to both of us, Remi? What about our company? You have to stay back, if anything, to organize all of this. You're good behind the curtain, and I want to take advantage of that. As for you, Del, I believe that you might create trouble if you came with us."

"I'm not an idiot," Del muttered.

"I never said you were. But Angus is your mate, correct?"

Del hesitated, then nodded. "Yes."

"What happens if you see someone touching him inappropriately? What if someone tries to grab him?"

"I'd step in and stop them, but if he's your pet, no one should be touching either of you."

Ryland grinned. "It's nice that you're trying to convince yourself and me of that, but we both know it's bullshit. I wouldn't be surprised if you broke a few jaws and growled at anyone who looks at Angus in a way they shouldn't."

"The two of you are out," Cam said. "But I still think Ryland should have at least one human bodyguard. Would a man like him and like the other people buying shifters fully trust shifters to keep him safe?"

"I'll go, then," Matt declared.

"You're not trained."

"Then I can be Ryland's personal assistant. Surely someone as rich as him and all that bullshit would have one."

Del's head looked like it was about to explode, and Angus didn't blame him. He hadn't expected Del's father to volunteer for this.

"And I have the perfect shifter to go with you," Cam said.

"Mercer is strong, and he teaches our recruits for pack security. He can get Matt into some kind of shape by the weekend."

"You can't do this," Del croaked, looking from Angus to his father.

Angus hated that he was hurting his mate, but this was non-negotiable. "I'll be fine," he promised, holding Del's gaze. "Your father will be there to keep me safe."

Del chuckled darkly. "Maybe, but who will keep *him* safe?"

Del couldn't believe Cam was agreeing to this or that his father had volunteered for it. He was pissed that everyone in the room was going along, and he got to his feet, ready to be done with this meeting.

He shouldn't have walked into it, to begin with. Maybe if he hadn't, he wouldn't have had to worry about his mate and his father.

"Del," Matt said as Del stomped past him.

Del shook his head. "Leave me alone. I can't believe you did this."

He rushed out in the hallway, needing to get out of the room and possibly the house. Toby walked out of the kitchen just as Del passed it and tried to talk to him, but Del shook his head and continued until he was outside. The front door slammed closed behind him, and he leaned against the porch railing, taking a deep breath and closing his eyes.

He breathed in and out, pushing the anger away. Maybe this was one of the reasons everyone had agreed he shouldn't go with Angus and Ryland. If he couldn't control himself in a safe situation, how could he hope to do so when everyone would be in danger?

So maybe he understood why he shouldn't be the one going with Angus and Ryland. Why should his father go, though?

Del's father wasn't a trained fighter. He was in good shape, and when he had time, he went to the gym and took martial arts lessons, but it didn't feel like enough. Beyond his family, Angus was the most precious person in Del's life. He needed his mate to be safe, and while he trusted his father to make sure nothing happened to Angus, he couldn't help but wonder how he was supposed to deal with worrying about his father and his mate getting killed.

"Del?" a voice asked from behind him.

Del screwed his eyes shut. He wasn't sure he was ready to talk to Angus, but apparently, he wouldn't have a choice. He didn't want to yell at Angus, even though that was his first instinct. He needed to look at this rationally, the way everyone else had.

After sucking in a breath, Del turned to face Angus. "I don't like any of what just happened," he said.

Angus nodded. He stepped out onto the porch and closed the door behind himself. It gave them some semblance of privacy, although Del could hear people talking inside the house.

"I wouldn't like it if our positions were reversed either," Angus said.

"Because I'm a weak human?"

"It has nothing to do with you being weak or human and everything to do with you being my mate and me worrying about something happening to you. I know you feel the same, which is why you tried to go with me, right?"

Del huffed. "I know it was a bad idea. I won't insist. I don't understand why my father is deemed good enough to go while I'm not, though."

"It's because your father doesn't worry and care about me as much as you do."

"We don't even know each other well," Del muttered.

Instead of offending Angus, it made him smile. "We don't, but I know you better than I know your father. I'd never even met him before today. Besides, this has nothing to do with knowing each other and everything to do with our bond. It doesn't matter how long we've been together. The bond between us is strong, and it'll push you to do something stupid if it means helping me."

Del would have to take Angus's word for that. As a human, he couldn't feel the bond between them, and it had no effect on him beyond making him want to spend as much time as possible with Angus. He didn't care much about it, just like he didn't care about whether or not the bond was pushing him to fall in love with Angus. He just knew he was and didn't want anything to happen to his mate.

"You can't forbid me to do things, though," Angus said. "I understand the bond between us is strong and that you're worried, but I'm still an adult. I can make my own decisions, especially when it comes to this. This situation, the mission and finding the shifters and the people auctioning them is important to me. I need to see it through."

Del rubbed his face. He should have known better than to tell Angus he couldn't do it. He'd have told Angus to fuck off if Angus had tried doing the same with him. The only person who'd ever been able to tell Del what to do was his father, and with Del being twenty, he hadn't done that in a while.

"I apologize for that," Del said. "I shouldn't have, and I don't think I would have normally. I panicked. I don't want to lose you, especially not so soon after finding you."

Angus stepped forward. "I accept your apology, and I understand. We both said things we might not have said otherwise and didn't mean. The situation is putting everyone on edge, including both of us." He reached for one of Del's hands and linked their fingers together. "As long as you don't try to order me around again, we can forget all about this."

But could they? Because Angus was still in danger, and now, so was Del's father.

Del was still panicking. He loved his father and was terrified of something happening to him, and he was falling fast and hard for Angus. He didn't understand why or how it worked, but he didn't want it to stop. He wanted so much more with Angus, and none of that would happen if the mission went wrong.

He cleared his throat. "How about we agree that neither of us can order the other to do or not do something as long as we talk about big decisions like this one?" he suggested. "I understand why you want to do it, and my reaction was knee-jerk. I should have allowed you to explain better, although I'm not sure that even if you had, I would have agreed to this. I don't, and I'm sure you're aware of that."

Angus grinned. "You made it pretty clear."

"You're still going to go through with it."

"I am. I need to do this."

"Then I'll stop bitching about it and support you. Just, next time, maybe talk to me first? I broke down in front of everyone, and I hate that."

"I promise that I'll talk to you first next time." Angus moved even closer. Del was pretty sure this was closer than they'd been since they'd met. His heart raced. It wasn't because of fear this time, but rather because of anticipation and want.

"And you'll talk to me before making big decisions," Angus continued. "That includes moving and what you want to do with your life and your future."

Del had hinted at the fact that he wasn't sure college was still for him, and Angus hadn't judged him for it. He'd given him support, which was what Del had needed and still needed now.

"I'm not used to talking with anyone," Angus murmured.

"I don't have family, and I barely have friends. I've always been independent because I had to be, so sometimes, I might forget that I promised to talk to you. I hope you won't hold it against me."

"How could I? We'll both do our best with this relationship, and that's all I expect." And for Angus to stay behind, but that wasn't going to happen.

"Learning to be in a relationship with someone is hard, but I think especially so when that someone is your mate. There's so much that could break between us and ruin everything that I'm almost afraid to do the things I want the most."

"Like what?" Del was pretty sure they weren't talking about the mission anymore.

Angus tilted his head to look at him. "Do you know how long I've wanted to kiss you?"

"If your feelings for me are anywhere close to my feelings for you, it's since the first time we met."

"It is."

Angus's confirmation was all Del needed. He cupped one of Angus's cheeks with his free hand and leaned forward, so close that his and Angus's breath mingled.

Then he kissed Angus.

It was everything Del had imagined it would be, but also more. Kissing Angus, feeling his lips against his, his taste, made Del feel like he'd come home. It was odd, and it had never happened to him before, but he was glad for that. Angus was the only person who was his home. He was Del's future and would become his everything in time.

As long as they both gave their bond and each other a chance.

# CHAPTER FOUR

A ngus felt ridiculous. He usually spent his days in front of his computer, wearing jeans and t-shirts, but today, he had on light flowy pants and a vest that left his chest bare.

He felt ridiculous.

It didn't matter that Del was looking at him as if he was the most beautiful man in the world. If Angus had a choice, he'd cover himself up, then hide in his office for the rest of the day.

"Do I really have to wear this?" he asked no one in particular.

"I tried to convince Remi to let you wear a t-shirt, but he nixed the idea," Ryland answered.

He was wearing a suit and looked perfectly at ease in it. Angus understood why he shouldn't be dressed the same way, and he didn't *want* to wear a suit, but there had to be something better than the pants and vest.

He looked at Remi, ready to beg, but Remi didn't even let him speak.

"Ryland already has bodyguards. That's not why you're there."

"I know we're hoping people will presume what my role is in Ryland's life, but do I really have to expose so much skin? I feel ridiculous." Angus plucked at the vest. "I can't believe the other shifters there will be dressed the same way."

"Some of them will. Some will wear even less. If this is too hard for you to deal with, you need to tell us now."

Angus swallowed and shook his head. He knew this was the only way to make the mission happen. He could complain all he wanted, but at the end of the day, he'd do it, and he'd do it with a smile on his face. He was only acting, but the other shifters he'd meet tonight wouldn't be. He'd do everything he could to free them and ensure they wouldn't be hurt again.

Unfortunately, that meant he'd have to keep himself in check at least tonight and that he'd have to wear ridiculous clothes.

"You don't have to go if you don't feel up for it," Del said from the corner of the room.

After getting dressed, they'd all met in Cam's office. Mercer and Matt were there, too, and like Ryland, they wore suits. Theirs were black and didn't look as if they'd cost more than Angus made in a month, but still. They were handsome, and no one would look at them and think Ryland had bought them at an auction.

"I'll do it," Angus said, defying Del with his gaze.

They hadn't talked about this again. They'd only had a few days to prepare, and Angus hadn't wanted to make things even more awkward between them. They'd both agreed that they needed to talk about big decisions, but also that they had to let the other do what he felt was for the best. Del hadn't tried changing Angus's mind, but Angus didn't doubt that he would if he could.

He wasn't okay with Angus putting himself in danger. It didn't matter that he hadn't said anything about it again and that he probably wouldn't. Angus and he both knew his feelings, and Angus was having a hard time dealing with them.

Before, he hadn't had to think twice about making decisions. He was the only one involved, and it had been freeing. Now, whenever he needed to do something, he thought about Del. He couldn't avoid doing so and didn't want to. Del was in his life to stay, and in the end, that was all that mattered.

But it wasn't easy. They were both learning their boundaries and limits and how to be together, and it was still unsteady. It felt like something might break with every single thing Angus said or did, and he didn't like that feeling.

"If everyone's ready, we should head out," Remi said.

He was still pissed about not going with Ryland, and he'd accepted it as gracefully as Del had accepted that Angus would be doing this. There was a lot of grumbling and glaring, but like everyone else, he was doing his job, which was organizing everything behind the scene.

Everyone moved toward the door. Angus was the last one to get there, but Del was right in front of him, and he stopped moving once they were alone in the room. He turned to face Angus, and they stared at each other for a moment.

"I'll be fine," Angus said.

He didn't promise it because he wasn't sure he could keep that promise, but he hoped he'd come home in one piece.

Del nodded. "I know. My father will protect you."

When he'd seen Matt train with Mercer, Angus had been impressed with his capability. They'd only had a few days, and Angus had been forced to refresh his self-defense moves. He wasn't any better at it than he'd been before, but it might give him the upper hand if he needed one.

Matt had been great, though. He'd taken Angus to the side one day and had promised him that he'd keep him safe. He was doing this for his son's sake, and keeping Angus safe would mean that Del was happy. That was all Matt wanted and the only reason he'd volunteered for this.

"He will, and I'm not unable to take care of myself."

"I'm not worried about you not taking care of yourself. Your body isn't the only way someone can hurt you, Angus. I'm terrified of what seeing those shifters at the auction will do to you."

Angus couldn't say he wasn't worried, but he still had to do this. "I'll be fine," he repeated.

"I hope so."

Del dragged him into his arms, and for a moment, nothing existed beyond the two of them. Angus was able to forget about the auction, the party, and the clothes he was wearing. He breathed in his mate's scent, knowing that soon, he'd be back in Del's arms.

He had to be.

They didn't say anything else when they separated. They'd already talked, and it wouldn't be useful for them to waste more time. Instead, they finally headed outside, where everyone else was waiting for them.

Del would be going with Remi. They'd be staying outside the place where the party was held, ready to intervene if something happened. They wouldn't be the only ones present, either. A few pack members had volunteered, including Doyle's mate Marcus and Carey. Carey was a phoenix shifter, and he'd seemed way too excited about the prospect of kicking ass.

But Angus, Ryland, and the others would be protected, whatever happened.

"Ready to go?" Ryland asked as he moved closer to Angus.

Angus nodded. He was nervous, but he knew what he had to do.

Everything he'd need was hidden under his clothing. If there was one good thing to be said about loose clothes, it was that it was fairly easy to hide things under them. Ryland had offered to carry everything for Angus, but Angus felt better having it on himself.

Ryland guided Angus toward the limousine they'd use for the night. Mercer and Matt followed, sitting in the front, with Mercer at the wheel. The door closed behind Angus, the noise sounding final and heavy.

"You'll be fine," Ryland said. "Even if Mercer and Matt are busy, I can protect you. I did create a private security company, after all."

"My safety isn't what I'm worried about." It was only part of it.

Ryland's smile faded. "It's not the only thing I'm worried about, either."

They were silent after that. Luckily, it seemed like most of the people involved in the auctions were local, so it didn't take them long to reach the place where the party was held, just over half an hour. Ryland didn't do or say anything during that time, but Angus kept bouncing his knee and looking out the window.

Once they reached the building, which looked like nothing interesting from the outside, Mercer and Matt sprang into action. They led Ryland and Angus out, then toward the building. Ryland offered Angus his arm, and Angus took it, grateful for the reassuring contact. He wouldn't have to say or do anything specific right now. He needed to act as if he was Ryland's property, and property didn't speak.

"My invitation?" Ryland asked when they reached the door.

He didn't sound like himself anymore, which was kind of scary and made Angus shiver. Ryland noticed and wrapped an arm around Angus's shoulders, lightly kissing his temple. "Relax," he whispered.

Angus dared look up. Two massive men framed the door, and one of them was talking with Mercer. He was checking the invitation Angus had created, and Angus held his breath as he waited to see if it would work.

It did.

The man checking the invitation nodded at the other, who opened the door and gestured them in. Mercer went first, then Ryland and Angus, and finally, Matt.

The inside of the building couldn't have been any more different from the outside.

Outside, it had been plain and gray, nothing more than a

big box. Inside, it dripped with gold and luxury. Everywhere Angus looked, he saw marble floors, expensive wooden furniture, and people dressed as if they were millionaires.

They probably were.

"Ready?" Ryland asked.

Angus squeezed Ryland's waist with his arm in answer. This was it. They were doing it, and while Angus couldn't wait to get out of here, he had work to do and was more than ready to do it.


Del was starting to wonder if insisting on coming along had been a good idea. The only one inside not wearing a camera and microphone was Angus, but between Mercer, Matt, and Ryland, Del could see and hear everything Angus was seeing and hearing.

And he hated it.

The five of them were crammed into the back of the van parked a few streets away from where the party was being held. There wasn't a lot of room to move or breathe, but Del was focused on the screens in front of him anyway. From the cameras the men inside were wearing, he could see dozens of elegantly dressed people moving around. Some of them were alone, although most had at least one man dressed in a suit hovering by their shoulder, no doubt a bodyguard.

Then there were the shifters.

Most of them were dressed similarly to Angus, some even more skimpily. It was clear they weren't here because they wanted to be, although some wore neutral expressions. A few others were clearly pissed, others seemed tired, and even more looked terrified. Del wished he could help every single one of them, and he had to work hard to stay where he was instead of rushing out and doing something stupid.

"How are you feeling?" Doyle asked.

He'd snuck in right before they left, to Remi's displeasure. Del was glad for his brother's presence, though. He was the only one here he knew well and the only one he could talk to.

"I've been better," he confessed.

Doyle snorted softly. "I bet you have. I'm sorry you have to go through this."

"It's fine."

"It's really not. I'm impressed, though. Your mate is a force of nature, and when he wants something, he takes it."

"Even though he might get hurt," Del muttered.

On the screens, he could see people mingling, talking, and drinking champagne. A couple of men stepped way too close to Angus, and Del was ever more thankful for Mercer and his father, who always managed to keep those men away.

One reached for Angus's face, but Ryland was quick to interrupt the action. He pulled Angus closer to his body, something Del had never thought he'd be grateful for.

"No touching," Mercer said with a growl.

The man raised both hands and took a step back. He was smiling, but Del was ready to bet he was annoyed. "I apologize. Most people don't mind if we touch their shifters."

"Well, I do," Ryland said smoothly. "I buy them for myself, not for others to touch."

"I understand. I don't think I've ever seen you at one of these parties before."

Del held his breath, but he shouldn't have worried. Ryland was smooth. "I haven't. This isn't how I usually find my shifters, but a friend of a friend talked to me about this opportunity, and I thought I'd see what it was about. I got an invitation if that's what you're worried about."

"Of course not. I was just curious as to who you are."

"I'm Ryland Young. You are?"

The man stared at Ryland for a moment before offering him his hand. "Colbert Smith."

Del wondered if that was Colbert's actual last name, but he honestly didn't care. Everly would look into it. He was back home in pack territory, hearing and seeing the same things Del and the others were. Del had no doubt he was already working on it.

Ryland looked around. "Security is impressive, although I would have done a few things differently," he commented.

"You know something about security?"

"I own a security company."

"I see. Maybe we can talk about all of this during dinner after the auction. I'm always open to adding more associates to my business opportunities."

"I'd be delighted."

Del swallowed. His stomach churned, threatening to make him throw up. He was disgusted by the way Colbert behaved. He acted as if shifters were nothing more than objects to be bought and sold. He wasn't one bit bothered about anything happening in that room, and Del counted backward from twenty to keep himself from going right inside and punching the asshole.

He peeked at his brother. Doyle was much calmer than he was, and while that might have something to do with the fact that Doyle's mate wasn't in there being treated like a piece of meat, Del couldn't help but be impressed.

His brother had always been the nervous kind, even when there was nothing to be nervous about. Right now, though, he was settled, and part of that was thanks to the man sitting next to him with his arm wrapped around his waist. Marcus had done Doyle a lot of good, but then, so had living with the pack. Doyle had finally found a place where he belonged, even though it had been hard in the beginning considering the situation that had brought him to the Rosewood pack.

"They're all doing great jobs," Doyle said as if he felt Del needed to be reassured.

"It's not the four of them I'm worried about. It's everyone else. What if they find out Angus and the others don't belong there?"

"Then we go in."

"It's that easy?"

Doyle nodded, suddenly serious. "Why else would we be here? We even brought Carey."

Del eyed the man. He was on the other side of the van, for which Del was grateful because he didn't seem to be able to stay still for more than a few seconds at a time. "What's up with him?"

"He's just a weird guy. You'll get used to it."

"Will I?"

Doyle grinned. "Just make sure to stay away from him when he gets into a fight. I wouldn't want you to burn to a crisp."

Del squinted at his brother. "That seems specific."

"Because it is. Carey and his twin brother are phoenix shifters. They can set things on fire with a thought, and Carey is way too enthusiastic about that, especially in fights. He tends to get carried away."

"I'll stay away from him," Del promised. Now that he knew what Doyle was talking about, he was happy to do so.

"Have you and Angus talked?" Doyle asked.

Del looked around the van. It would be impossible for the others not to hear what he was saying, but they were all focused on the screens. He supposed he should be, too, but it was hard to see Angus do this without him. It was for the best, though, and he'd realized that as soon as he and Angus had talked about it after the meeting with Ryland and Remi a few days ago.

That didn't mean he didn't want to run in there and protect his mate.

"How do you deal with these feelings?" he asked his

brother.

Doyle didn't ask what he was talking about. "It's tough, isn't it? And I bet it's even worse for you, considering the situation Angus is in right now."

"It's almost as if my brain isn't mine anymore. I've never felt this way for anyone else, and it's fucking confusing."

"It's still confusing for me, even though Marcus and I have been together for some time. I don't know if this feeling will ever smooth out, but I also don't know if I want it to. I like feeling this way. I like being nuts about Marcus and wanting to be with him all the time."

"What about when he's at work? Aren't you worried something will happen to him?"

"Always, but I have faith in him." He leaned closer. "Does this mean you're giving Angus a chance?"

Del looked at the screen. He was watching the party through Ryland's camera, which meant he could see Angus. Angus's expression was smooth, but his focus jumped from one person to another, and Del had no doubt he was working hard to keep up the show. He'd be fine, just like the others would.

"Was there ever a doubt I would?" he asked. "We'll see where things go after this, but I want it to work."

"It will," Doyle promised.

Del couldn't help but wonder if his brother was right. He wasn't lying, though. He'd do everything to make sure his relationship with Angus was successful.

"Something's happening," Remi suddenly said. He leaned even closer to the screen he was watching, his nose almost brushing against it.

Del did the same. He watched as Ryland and Angus were herded toward a door at the back of the room. The hallway they stepped in was dark, but Del could see curtains framing doors every few feet on the right side. Someone quickly brought them to one of the red curtains, which they raised. Behind the curtains were several comfortable-looking seats on what appeared to be some kind of balcony, and Ryland settled in one of them while Angus sat next to him. Mercer and Matt were no doubt behind them, making sure no one snuck in.

From this position, Del could see what Ryland saw, and it made his mouth go dry.

It was a stage framed by more red curtains and illuminated by one single spotlight directed right at the center of it.

The auction was about to begin.


Angus had to work hard not to throw up. He stared in front of him, wondering if he was strong enough not to run away screaming or possibly jump onto the stage and intervene.

Ryland grabbed his hand and squeezed. Angus was thankful for the relative darkness. Otherwise, he wouldn't have been able to fool anyone into thinking he was a meek shifter only doing what his master wanted.

"This is awful," Ryland murmured.

Angus suspected he was holding onto him for both their sakes. Knowing that Ryland's brother had been involved in something like this couldn't be easy for Ryland. Angus despised how these shifters were treated, but he didn't have a personal connection to any of them. The same couldn't be said for Ryland, yet, he hadn't hesitated to come on this mission.

"Do we know what's going to happen?" Matt asked.

"Not for sure, but I can imagine," Angus told him.

The silence between them was tense as they waited. It took several more minutes for the room to fall quiet. The only light was the spotlight on the stage, but it was so bright that Angus could see the other balconies. The people he'd seen earlier sipping champagne and talking were eagerly staring at the stage.

One woman was even leaning so far out over the railing that he wondered if she might be about to fall.

One could hope.

Then a man stepped onto the stage. A scattering of applause made Angus want to rage, but instead, he swallowed and looked at the man. Like every other human in the room, he wore a suit that appeared to be costly enough to pay for Angus's grocery shopping for an entire year. He held the microphone and stopped right under the spotlight, seeming to love it. He raised his free hand and waved at a few people, and Angus took advantage of that moment to examine him.

The man had to be in his early fifties, possibly a bit older. His hair was dark, though, making Angus wonder if he dyed it. That was probably the case, but his mustache betrayed his age, with the silver strands in it glinting under the light. The man had a strong nose and was dressed impeccably. He gave off an air of being rich, which he had to be to be present tonight.

"Is that our host?" Ryland asked.

"I'm sure *they're* already on it," Mercer murmured to him.

"Welcome back," the man said. "Since I've been warned there are new faces tonight, let me introduce myself. My name is Fulton, as most of you are aware of. I'm the organizer of this party and auction, and please, if I don't know you yet, come to me once it's over. I want *all* my guests to be happy with what they find at the auction and with the food and drinks. Besides, I always look forward to getting to know new people."

Someone tittered, and Angus glared around. Ryland's hand tightened on his, and he leaned forward, expecting what was about to happen.

Angus dreaded it. It would be the hardest part of all of this. He'd have to watch shifters being auctioned without being able or allowed to do anything to help them.

"Programs with the names and details of the shifters about to go on auction are being distributed right now," Fulton continued. "Please, take a few minutes to go over them and make your choice. I hope everyone will find something they want and will enjoy, although, of course, the only way to win who you want is by using your credit card."

A smattering of laughter made Angus grit his teeth. He wasn't a violent person, but right now, he wished he could kill every single person in the room.

Fulton bowed lightly. "Enjoy your evening, and I'll see you later, during dinner."

Fulton left the stage, and the noise level went up again. Angus was relieved—it would hide whatever he and the others had to say—but the anticipation made him sick.

There was a movement behind them, but Mercer stepped in before Angus could see what was happening. He quietly talked to someone, and when the curtain lowered again, he appeared next to Ryland, holding what looked like a thin booklet. He appeared disgusted as he held it out to Ryland with two fingers, but Ryland didn't hesitate to snatch it from him.

He let go of Angus's hand and quickly thumbed through the leaflet. Angus knew the moment he realized his brother wouldn't be auctioned tonight. Ryland's shoulders slumped, and he let out a heavy sigh.

"We knew this might be a possibility," Angus told him.

"I know. I was still hoping he'd be here."

Angus understood, so he left Ryland alone. Ryland continued looking through the leaflet, but Angus couldn't help but notice that he paused at one page in particular. He wondered if maybe Ryland knew whoever the shifter on that page was, but the room fell silent before he could ask.

Someone had appeared on stage, and it wasn't Fulton. He was still there, standing to the side, holding his microphone, looking like a kid in a toy shop at Christmas, but he wasn't the center of attention anymore.

"Our first item is a twenty-six-year-old unicorn shifter," he said, watching a woman being chained to a hook at the center of the stage.

She wore just enough to hide her breasts and her private parts. She folded her arms around her and looked around, but Angus suspected she couldn't see much because of the darkness of the room and the brightness of the light on stage. She was blonde, and her hair hung around her face, making her look like an angel.

Unfortunately for her, she wasn't.

Angus tuned out while she was being auctioned. He clutched the arms of his seat, keeping himself anchored there so he wouldn't do something stupid. He was glad when the woman disappeared from the stage, but she was replaced by a man who couldn't be much older than eighteen, if even that, and it was almost enough to send him running to the stage.

A hand landed on his shoulder. He turned around to see that Matt was looking down at him rather than at the stage, and he was grateful that his father-in-law had stopped him from doing something stupid.

"Thank you," he said.

Matt nodded. His expression was hard, and Angus realized they were in very much the same state. They both wanted to intervene, but they couldn't.

The next man looked even younger, although Fulton made sure to explain he was in his mid-twenties. It didn't seem possible, given how tiny the man was.

"Now, this one is special," Fulton drawled. "I know that by looking at him and how small he is, you'd never think it, but Tyler here is a gargoyle shifter."

Murmurs in the crowd told Angus several people were interested. He could understand why. Gargoyle shifters were incredibly rare, and Tyler was adorable to boot. He was short and slight, and he looked like a fragile cherub with his messy blond hair. There was something to Tyler's face that made him look barely adult.

Angus's stomach churned with disgust at the thought of what the people who bought him would do to him. He wanted nothing more than to protect Tyler, even more so than he'd wished for the other shifters that had been auctioned tonight.

"Let's start with a hundred thousand dollars," Fulton said.

The offer was taken up, but whoever had bid wasn't the only one interested. Angus gritted his teeth, waiting for the auction to be over, dreading what would happen to Tyler when it was.

He was stunned when Ryland raised one of his hands. "Five hundred thousand dollars," he declared.

Mercer grumbled behind him, but Ryland didn't seem to care or even hear him. He kept his focus straight on the stage, locked on Tyler, who was trying to hide his body with his arms with little success, since he was only wearing a pair of tight white briefs.

Fulton looked around, squinting as if to find out who was offering so much money for a shifter. "I don't think I recognize that voice," he said.

"You don't have to recognize it," Ryland snapped. "Is the shifter mine?"

Fulton chuckled. "We'll find out soon enough. Does someone offer five hundred fifty thousand dollars?" he asked, looking around.

No one did. That meant that Ryland had just bought Tyler, and Angus had no idea whether or not it was a good thing when it came to their mission. He also didn't care—Tyler was safe, and that was all that mattered.

"What the fuck is he doing?" Remi muttered.

His focus was stuck on the screens, and Del didn't blame him. He wanted to ask Ryland what he was doing, too. Why had he bought that guy? Had he played all of them and gotten a way in the auction for that?

"He's trying to help," Doyle murmured.

"By buying a guy?" Remi was angry.

Del didn't blame him. Ryland was putting the entire operation in danger, even if he was doing this for a good reason. Angus was right there next to him, and Del prayed nothing would happen to him.

"By getting him out of there. Wouldn't you have done something if you'd been in his place?"

Remi sighed, and his shoulder slumped. "I wish he'd buy all these people, but we can't draw that much attention to us."

"Buying one guy isn't going to do that. If anything, it'll tell these people that Ryland is serious about all of this and that he has money to spare," Everly's voice said. He was back in Rosewood, but he was working the operation with them.

Del understood. As soon as he'd seen the first shifter being auctioned, he'd wanted to help her. He wouldn't have been able to buy her or any of the others, but every time one of them was bought, his heart broke a little more. It was a relief to know that at least this guy would be safe—as long as Ryland kept up his role as a rich asshole.

He watched as the auctions continued, but he couldn't focus. He was terrified for Angus, and it only got worse when the auction was over. It meant Angus and Ryland would have to mingle again, and Del didn't know how he'd be able to stand watching that.

He held his breath as Fulton stepped onto the balcony where Ryland and Angus had been sitting before they could leave.

"A new face," he drawled, ignoring Mercer and Matt.

He didn't ignore Angus, though. Angus stared at the floor as if he was afraid, but Del could see that wasn't true. He was angry and possibly afraid of what he'd do if Fulton tried talking to him.

"Where can I retrieve my purchase?" Ryland interjected, placing himself between Fulton and Angus.

Fulton chuckled. "Eager?"

"I paid half a million dollars for him, so yes. I'd like to take him home."

"And skip dinner?"

Del couldn't see Ryland's face anymore, but he could imagine his expression just by his tone of voice when he next spoke.

"I didn't come here to have dinner with people I don't know and couldn't care less about. I came here for the shifters, and now that I have one, I'm ready to head out."

"I can assure you that the food is perfect, as is the company. Most buyers stay to talk to other like-minded people, and business connections are often formed. Besides, if you're planning to attend more of my parties, maybe it would be good for you to get to know the others."

Del's mouth was dry. He needed Angus to get out of there. His skin crawled as he listened to the conversation and Fulton's voice. The man wasn't just an asshole. He sold people and became rich on their torture, and he clearly didn't care one bit about them.

"Take me to Tyler," Ryland ordered. He leaned closer to Fulton, but Del and the others could still hear him. "Now. I'll pick up my purchase and head out. If you want to talk about business, you're welcome to contact my company."

"Should I invite you to my next party?"

"Only if you have something interesting to sell."

Ryland reached back, and Del could see he took Angus's

hand. He dragged Angus along as he pushed past Fulton. Del expected the asshole to try to stop them, but instead, he said, "Take him to the cages and hand him his purchase. I'll see you soon, Mr. Young."

Since Ryland hadn't introduced himself, Fulton shouldn't know his name. He'd clearly looked into him, which wasn't surprising but still gave Del the creeps.

It was hard to breathe as Del looked at the screens at the progression Angus and Ryland made. They were taken away from the balconies and the auction area and into a more spartan hallway with gray cement walls and floors. From there, they entered a room that made Del swear and look away.

When Fulton had mentioned cages, he hadn't been lying. Two rows of them lined the walls, some empty, others containing the shifters who'd been auctioned. They were visibly scared and pressed against the back of their cages. Tyler was, too, when the group stopped in front of his.

His cage was open, but he didn't step out. Del wondered how they were going to do this for a moment, then sucked in a breath when Angus stepped forward. He looked straight at Tyler and offered him his hand, and after a moment of hesitation and a look behind Angus, Tyler took it. He allowed Angus to pull him out of the cage, and Del wasn't surprised to see his father slide out of his jacket and drape it over Tyler's shoulders. Tyler looked back at him and jerked as if surprised. His eyes were wide, but thankfully, he didn't try to run when Matt put a hand on his shoulder and guided him away.

Del was so tense he felt he might snap. He followed Angus's path on the screen, and as soon as they were at the exit, he shot out of his seat. Remi called out something, but Del didn't stop. He opened the back door of the van and rushed out. Even if Angus didn't need him, he'd be there for him, dammit.

Del wasn't the only one running toward the limo Ryland

and Angus had arrived in. Doyle was with him, silently supporting him. They reached the limo before the others, and Del slipped in. He wanted to go straight to Angus, but he knew better. No matter how much he wanted to help, exposing them would only make things worse.

Doyle had to hold him back when the limo door opened. Ryland slid in, his eyes widening when he saw Del and Doyle. Angus was right behind him, and Del was surprised not to see Tyler with him. Instead, Tyler was wrapped in Del's father's arms, wearing his too-long jacket.

Mercer made a disgusted sound when he looked back as he climbed into the driver's seat, but thankfully, he didn't say anything. He turned on the engine and drove off faster than he should.

Del grabbed Angus and pulled him into his lap. He wrapped his arms around him and buried his face against his mate's neck, telling himself that Angus was safe. He could touch him, feel him, and he was okay.

"Let's go home," Ryland said.

They did. It was late, so they didn't linger once they reached pack territory. They'd talk about the mission and how Del and Doyle had messed up tomorrow. The only problem was that Del wasn't ready to go home with his father and leave Angus behind, so he clung to him as Toby led Tyler inside to one of the guest rooms.

"Meeting tomorrow," Cam declared as he looked at their group.

"Thank fuck," Remi muttered. "You and I need to talk, Ry."

Ryland ignored him. "Will Tyler be okay?" he asked Cam.

"Yes. Go home, everyone."

Del didn't want to, so he took a risk. "Angus?"

Angus looked tired, but he smiled. "Yes?"

"Can I stay with you tonight?"

Angus stared for a moment. He didn't ask Del why he wanted to stay or what he had in mind. "Of course."

Del was so relieved that he could have kissed him. Instead, he said goodbye to his father, explained he'd be staying the night, and followed Angus to his bedroom. Neither of them spoke as Angus disappeared into the bathroom, no doubt to shower. After what he'd been through tonight, he'd need time to himself, so Del decided to give him that.

He felt awkward, but things didn't have to be that way. He doubted Angus would be up for much once he came out, so he went to work getting everything ready. That way, they could go to bed right away.

He turned down the bed and undressed. He hesitated, but they were going to sleep, and he didn't want to be uncomfortable, so he took off his jeans and his sweater and left them on the chair by the window. The light streaming through was soft but strong enough that he could move without bumping into anything.

He didn't want to presume anything, but it was clear they were about to share a bed, so he got under the blankets and pulled them up under his armpits. Then he waited.

It didn't take long for Angus to come out, and when he did, his hair was damp and he was only wearing a towel wrapped around his waist. That was all Del had time to see before Angus turned off the light.

"How tired are you?" Angus asked as he moved toward the bed.

"Not as much as you. I spent the night sitting on my ass." While Angus was in danger.

"I'm not tired. I didn't do much."

Del licked his lips when Angus unwound the towel from his waist and let it drop to the floor. He climbed into bed and settled next to Del, but they didn't touch.

Not yet.

Del was tense and had no idea what to do. Thankfully, his mate didn't seem to have that problem because he rolled toward Del and plastered their bodies together. The shock of his damp, cool body against Del's heated one was heaven, and Del opened his arms to welcome the man he was falling in love with.

Angus growled, stunning Del. It should have sounded corny, even coming from a shifter, but it sent a shiver down Del's spine instead. Angus had been hesitant in their relationship, but then, so was Del. That Angus was gone now, though, and all that was left was a man who knew what he wanted — Del.

Del opened his legs. Instead of taking advantage of that, Angus rolled away. Del heard the sound of a drawer opening, then closing, and Angus was back, solid and perfect on top of Del.

They rolled together until they almost fell out of bed, and Angus was under Del. He slapped the bottle of lube he'd grabbed from the drawer on Del's chest, telling him what he wanted without a word.

Del grinned and smoothed his palms down Angus's side, then around them until he could cup Angus's ass. He slipped a finger between the still-damp cheeks and teased Angus's hole with the tip of a finger.

Angus stretched under Del and opened the lube Del hadn't taken from him yet. He squirted some on his fingers and looked at Del in question. Del rolled them again, making Angus grin. He didn't care how they did this, but in this position, it would be easier for Angus to have access either to his ass or to Del's.

Angus sat up, straddling Del's hips. He reached back, and while Del couldn't see what he was doing, he had a great imagination. Angus's expression helped him with that, too, but he still ran his fingertips around Angus's waist until he met

Angus's hand. He followed it to Angus's fingers. Lust tore through him when he realized Angus already had two of them in his ass, and he pushed one of his right along with them.

Angus leaned forward and pressed his forehead against Del's shoulder. "You're perfect."

Del barked out a laugh. "Not really."

"Okay, maybe not, but you're damn close. That's enough for me."

"Yeah?" Del needed it to be

He and Angus moved in sync, getting Angus ready. Del loved that his mate included him in this. It would have been easier to take care of it himself, but they were in this together.

"Yeah. I couldn't have asked for a better mate."

Del hoped Angus wouldn't regret those words in a few months. Even if he did, though, they were mates, and Del had learned that it meant a lot to shifters.

"Come on, Del. Fuck me," Angus whined.

Del pushed his hand between them and grabbed his dick, holding it up so Angus could sink onto it.

Leaning back, Angus gripped Del's thighs almost too hard as he did so, making Del groan at the pinch of pain. He closed his eyes and swallowed, hanging onto his control.

Angus sat down, his ass pressing against Del's thighs.

They were one. It wouldn't last long—there was no way Del would be able to stop himself from coming—but it was perfection. He hadn't known he wanted this, but now he couldn't imagine his life without Angus.

Del shifted his hips. Angus looked down at him with heated eyes that told Del what he wanted. They just stared at each other for a moment, and Del knew this was his future.

Angus was his future.

Then Angus rose and sank down again. His eyes rolled back as he dropped his head and bit his lips, never looking away. It wasn't the first time Del had sex, but it was the most intimate one.

"I thought you were going to fuck me?" Angus asked.

Del laughed. "I will."

All thoughts of the future could wait.

Del pressed his feet against the mattress and pushed his hips up. Angus yelped and leaned down to put his hands on Del's shoulders. He used the hold to help his movements, and while it took a moment for them to coordinate, eventually, they got it.

Angus grinned down.

Del had never wanted anything more than this — than Angus. And now, he had it. He had *everything*.

Suddenly, this wasn't tender anymore. That was good with Del. because he felt like he was about to explode.

He flipped them, pushing Angus to his back and taking control. His hips moved instinctively as he yearned for the pleasure that was about to come, but he still made sure that Angus was right there with him.

Within minutes, he was ready to come. From the whimpers coming from Angus, he suspected he wasn't the only one, so he tilted his hips and kissed his mate. It took a few tries, but when he managed to nail Angus's prostate, Angus's back arched. He clung to Del as if trying to become part of him, but he already was. He'd been in Del's heart since the first time they met.

A wave of pleasure flooded Del when Angus's ass tightened around him. Angus shuddered and cried out. His nails dug into Del's shoulders, but Del barely felt it, because he was coming inside his mate, and it was the most perfect instant he'd ever experienced.

Del stopped moving. He pressed his forehead to Angus's, letting their breaths mingle as they both panted. He never wanted to move, and since he didn't wish to squash Angus, he held himself up on his elbows. His muscles felt weak, so it wouldn't last forever, but for now, he couldn't let go of Angus.

He didn't have to. Angus had found him, and he was never leaving him. Knowing that no matter what happened, they'd always have each other, Del finally allowed himself to relax in a way he hadn't done in years.

He was safe and loved. He had a home, and he'd found his place in the world.

Finally.

# CHAPTER FIVE

When Angus woke up with Del in his bed, he wished he could stay there the entire day. After the auction last night, he felt he deserved it, but unfortunately, their team already had plans. There was a meeting in Cam's office in an hour, and Angus needed to be there.

He didn't want to talk about the auction, but there was no way out of it, even though anyone could see the video of what had happened. Besides, Angus wanted to check in on Tyler, who'd been through a lot and no doubt didn't trust anyone, especially not Ryland. It would take him a while to realize they truly had no intention of hurting him or even keeping him in Rosewood, but in the meantime, Angus wanted him to see a friendly face. Tyler had believed Angus was an auctioned shifter like himself, so maybe, he'd trust him.

"Good morning," Del said, smiling from his side of the bed.

Angus snuggled against him. "Good morning."

"Is it already time to get up?"

"Unfortunately, at least if we both want a shower. The meeting is in an hour."

Del sighed and kissed Angus's forehead. "I want to check in on my father, but if I didn't, I'd stay in bed with you the entire day."

His words made Angus smile, since he'd been thinking the same seconds ago. He kissed Del's chest, then sat up. "I get the first shower."

"We could shower together," Del offered.

"But if we do, we'll be distracted, and we'll be late." And

Angus didn't want that to happen. Tyler was in another guest room, somewhere down the hall, no doubt terrified. He needed Angus, and Angus wanted to be there for him.

He showered, then left Del in his room as he headed to the kitchen. He wasn't surprised that Matt and Mercer were already there, both of them sipping coffee while quietly talking to Cam. They all looked up when they heard Angus, and Cam was gesturing at the coffee pot.

"There's enough coffee for everyone."

"Even Remi when he gets here?"

Cam chuckled. "I might have told him to get some coffee on the way, because I wasn't sure the machine could keep up with him. We should be fine, though."

Angus was grateful for the cup of coffee and took a few seconds to sip and relax. He couldn't help but worry about what was next, though. "Should I go fetch Tyler?" he asked.

"Will he want to be at the meeting?" Cam asked.

"There's only one way for us to know." Angus set down his coffee and headed back toward the hallway.

His bedroom door was closed, so Del was still getting ready. That was fine because it would give Angus some time to talk to Tyler.

He knocked on Tyler's door and waited for the gargoyle shifter to answer. He was curious about what gargoyle shifters could do, but he doubted that asking outright would help Tyler feel more comfortable. Angus could wait, and he would.

The door creaked open, and a pair of blue eyes peeked through. Angus smiled, keeping his expression relaxed. "Hi. I don't know if you remember me from last night, but my name is Angus."

The door opened just a bit more, enough to reveal Tyler. He looked like he hadn't slept, which might be the case. He was wearing a pair of too-big sweatpants and a t-shirt, both of them borrowed. It was better than the tiny white briefs he'd been wearing yesterday evening.

"You were with the man who bought me," Tyler said.

Angus couldn't deny that. "I was. How are you feeling?"

"Confused."

That made Angus smile. "I would be too, if I were in your shoes. Do you want to come with me to the kitchen? We're having a meeting over what happened last night, and we'd like your input."

"Will he be there?"

Angus wasn't sure who Tyler was talking about, but he assumed it was Ryland. "Ryland will be there, but even though he bought you, he's not a bad person. He just wanted to help you."

Tyler frowned. "That's what they all say, but he's not who I was talking about. His bodyguard. Will he be there?"

"They're both already there."

Angus hadn't missed the way Matt had taken care of Tyler as soon as he'd been delivered to them, so maybe he was the man Tyler was asking about. Telling him both Matt and Mercer were there was enough to get him to step out of his bedroom.

Angus didn't take him to the kitchen right away. He wanted Tyler to know nothing would happen to him, and while he realized that telling him wouldn't help him believe it, it was the first step. "Everyone here wants to protect you, including Ryland. I know we didn't tell you much yesterday, but you'll learn more during the meeting. Just know that Ryland's brother was taken, and he's been looking for him ever since. I think you remind him of him. That's why he bought you, but you're free, even though he paid a lot of money for you."

Tyler nodded. He kept looking up and down the hallway, maybe for an escape or a threat. Angus made sure not to touch him as he made his way toward the kitchen, Tyler right behind him. They walked in, and once again, everyone looked up. To everyone's surprise, Tyler made a beeline for Matt.

Today, Matt was wearing jeans and a sweater. He was leaning against the counter and smiled at Tyler when he saw him. His eyes widened when Tyler grabbed the edge of his sweater and held on, standing closer than most people would. He clearly had no idea what to do with Tyler, and Angus didn't blame him.

Since Tyler seemed to be okay, Angus took out a phone from his pocket. He'd cloned Colbert's phone yesterday when he was close enough, and while he hadn't had the time or inclination to go through the data yesterday, he was curious now. He focused on that as more people kept arriving, and the meeting moved to Cam's office.

Tyler was still holding onto Matt, but Matt didn't seem inclined to push him away. Angus was curious about the situation, but thankfully, neither he nor anyone else asked about it.

"So, what did we find out yesterday?" Cam asked from his seat behind his desk. "Apart from the fact that some people are monsters."

"I cloned Colbert's phone," Angus said. "But it'll take me a while to go through everything. So far, I have a long list of names and several files that look financial. It should help us find out more about who's behind the auctions and how to find the shifters they sell."

"Is there anything about my brother on there?" Ryland asked.

"Not that I was able to find, but I'm sure that if your brother was auctioned by these people, I'll find his name. Pembroke isn't common, after all."

Tyler sucked in a breath, and everyone in the room turned to him. He was standing next to Matt, who'd refused to sit down, and with everyone's attention on him, he shuffled his feet until he was half hiding behind Matt.

"Tyler?" Ryland asked.

Matt narrowed his eyes at him. He turned slightly, just enough to be able to look at Tyler. "Tyler? Do you recognize that name?"

Tyler hesitated, then nodded. "He's my friend."

Ryland made a strangled sound, but Remi was there to keep him where he was. Having him push Tyler would only freak Tyler out, which was the last thing anyone in the room needed.

"Can you tell me about Pembroke?" Matt asked.

Tyler was still clutching the bottom of Matt's sweater. He'd twisted his fingers into the fabric, holding on to him as if he were a child. It broke Angus's heart to see it, but he knew Matt would take care of Tyler.

"We were together," Tyler murmured softly enough that it was a struggle to hear him. "He's my best friend, and we lived together for a long time. But when our owner died, we were given to the people who sold me last night. Pembroke was sold before me, and I haven't seen him since. I don't know where he is now."

"Do you know who bought him?"

"A man called Colbert. I heard him boast about it."

This was it. Colbert had bought Pembroke, and Angus had what amounted to Colbert's phone in his hand. There *had* to be something in there that would lead them to Pembroke.

And once it did, they could rescue Pembroke and bring down the entire operation, just like they'd planned.

"We need to go now," Ryland declared.

Del wasn't surprised at his words. If they were talking about Doyle, he'd want to go to him right away, too. The problem was that Ryland was too deep into this. Pembroke was his brother, and after two years of looking for him, he'd finally found him. He wanted to get him back, but they needed to be careful. It would be too easy for someone to get hurt, or worse.

Thankfully, Del wasn't the only one who understood that. He could tell by Cam's expression that the alpha was about to say no, and he hoped Ryland wouldn't complicate the situation by doing or saying something stupid.

"We can't," Cam said.

"You told me you'd help me get my brother back," Ryland snapped. He got to his feet and paced the length of the office, which wasn't easy considering how many people were stuffed inside.

"I will. We all will."

"Then why are we talking about this? We should already be out there, headed toward this guy's house."

Del turned his attention to his father and Tyler. The shifter was still behind Del's father, looking warily at Ryland. Del understood. There was no way for him to know what Tyler had been through, but unfortunately, he had a good imagination. It wasn't surprising to find out he was afraid of people shouting and ranting.

What Del didn't understand was why Tyler had latched onto his father. Was it because he was human? That didn't make sense, because the people who'd hurt Tyler the most were humans. Besides, Matt hadn't been the only human present last night. Ryland had been there, too.

It would have made more sense for Tyler to trust shifters, but every time a shifter in the room moved, he pressed closer to Del's father. Del didn't mind. His father had made him feel safe his entire life, so he got it. He wanted Tyler to be okay and to feel comfortable, and if what he needed for that to happen was to be with Del's father, then Del was more than okay with that.

"We can't just barge in there," Remi pointed out. His voice was soft and gentle, as if he were afraid to hurt his friend. He probably was.

"Why not?" Ryland asked.

"Because someone could get hurt."

"I don't care if I get hurt. I only care about Pembroke."

"What if the person who gets hurt is him?"

That gave Ryland pause. He stopped in the middle of the room and stared at Remi.

"Remi's right," Cam said. "If I had my way, I'd go right now. I don't want anyone to be in Pembroke's position for a second longer than strictly necessary. It's not exactly the same, but my mate was a prisoner for a long time. Thinking about what he went through, even without being auctioned, makes me want to tear the world apart. We can't put anyone in danger, though, least of all Pembroke. Even if we find out where Colbert lives, we need to look into the blueprints of the house, the security system, the security company that works for him, and to be sure we can get to Pembroke. Rushing into this would only complicate things, and we can't afford for that to happen, especially not if we want to take down the entire operation."

"Unless you changed your mind about that," Angus said.

He'd spent most of the time Ryland had bitched about leaving right away on the phone. Del had no doubt he was working on Colbert's cloned phone already.

"I haven't," Ryland said.

Angus finally looked up. "Are you sure? Because no one would blame you. You agreed to help us so we'd find your brother, and we have. If you want out of this operation as soon as Pembroke is back with you, I'm sure we can find a way to make that happen."

Del wasn't as sure as Angus that that was the case. He was only marginally involved, but even he knew that they needed

Ryland's money and his security company. Without him, the operation would be a disaster, and they couldn't let that happen.

They needed Ryland to continue being involved.

Thankfully, Ryland shook his head. "I told you I wanted to take down the entire operation, and I will. *We* will."

"Then let us do our job. Let *me* do my job. I understand you want to help your brother right away. I do, too, especially after seeing what we saw last night. But we have no idea what we'd walk into, and I don't know about you, but I have no doubt that shifters are guarding the place. You never told us what kind of shifter your brother is, just that he's a rare shifter. What would Colbert use him for?"

Del hadn't been there in person yesterday, but he'd seen enough to understand that the humans who bought the shifters had different uses for them. Some of the shifters had been unicorn shifters, which meant they could heal people with their hands. Some shifters, like Tyler, could be good guards. He probably wouldn't do any good in his human form, but in his gargoyle form? Del didn't know a lot about rare shifters, but he knew enough. The kind of shifter one was impacted what was done with them.

And *to* them.

"He's a hydra shifter."

Del blinked. He hadn't expected that, but then, he hadn't expected Tyler to be a gargoyle shifter, either. As with every human, most of the shifters he knew were common, like wolves, bears, and big cats. He'd heard about rare shifters before moving to Rosewood, but those stories had always felt like they belonged in fairytale books rather than in reality. Finding out that unicorn and tiger shifters existed felt a bit like a dream, and Del couldn't believe he was in contact with these people every day and that they were as normal as he and his father.

"That's the dragon with three heads, right?" Angus asked.

Ryland nodded. "I don't know if I'd call him a dragon, but you get the idea, yes."

"Is it true that his heads grow again when they're cut off?"

Ryland's eyes narrowed. "I wouldn't know. I've never tried cutting my brother's head off."

"Right. Sorry. Anyway, considering that your brother's a hydra shifter, if I had to take a guess, I'd bet that Colbert uses him for security. It would make the most sense."

"Since when have bad guys made sense?" Remi muttered.

"You're not wrong, but we have to start somewhere. I have Colbert's phone cloned, but I don't know where to start looking, and poking around aimlessly hoping I'll find the right information, isn't doing much. Knowing the kind of task Pembroke was probably given will make my job easier, which means research will be easier and we won't have to wait as long as we would otherwise."

Ryland crossed his arms over his chest. "When do you think we'll be able to go?"

"I have no way to know. There's not much any of us can do for now except look through this phone. I'm sure Everly is already researching Colbert, Fulton, and anyone else involved he can identify. Once we know more about them and where they live, we'll be able to come up with a plan."

They talked for a while longer after that, but Angus was right. There was nothing any of them could do at the moment except for Angus and Everly, and repeating the same things, again and again, wouldn't help anyone. Ryland needed to put his energy into something productive, so Del was relieved when Remi told him they needed to get back to work. Del should train for a bit or maybe try to study, but he wasn't sure he'd be able to focus. Unfortunately, his college professors wouldn't care about what was happening in his personal life, and besides, it wasn't like he was about to tell them any of this.

Since Angus was busy, Del moved closer to his father. Tyler was still there, peeking around Matt, but he disappeared behind him again when he noticed Del.

Del frowned. Should he stay away from his father so he wouldn't scare Tyler?

Matt solved Del's dilemma by waving him closer. Tyler didn't look convinced, but Matt turned around and wrapped an arm around his shoulders, pulling him forward. "This is Del. He's my son, and you don't have to be afraid of him," he explained.

Tyler peered up at Del. "You were there last night."

"I was."

"Why?"

Del had no idea how to answer that, or rather, he did, but he wasn't sure it would help Tyler not be afraid of him. "Because my mate was there."

Tyler looked away from Del and at something behind him, and Del suspected that something was Angus. "You're a shifter's mate?" Tyler asked.

"I am."

"I didn't know that was possible," Tyler murmured.

His gaze strayed to Matt, and something in it took Del's breath away.

Yes, Tyler was terrified of what was happening to him and of the people around him, but Del suspected that wasn't why he clung to Matt the way he did.

But why did he, then?


Angus was only vaguely aware of what was happening around him. He was poking through the information he'd cloned from Colbert's phone, and while he kept an ear open on the meeting, he was busy.

Still, he wasn't so busy that he didn't notice when Tyler suddenly shifted.

Angus blinked, looking up. The last time he'd seen Tyler, he'd been clinging to Matt, and the two of them had been talking to Del. Del wasn't the one standing in front of them now, though. He was slightly to the side, looking alarmed as Tyler pushed Matt behind himself, clearly trying to protect him from Ryland.

"Everyone stop," Cam ordered.

Angus locked up the phone in his hand and pushed it into his pocket as he got to his feet. What was happening? He didn't know Ryland all that well, but he doubted the man would attack anyone, least of all Tyler and Matt.

Ryland raised his hands and stepped away from the two of them. "I apologize. I'm not sure what made Tyler react this way, but I mean no harm to him or Matt."

Angus stayed where he was, but Cam moved closer to the little group. Angus desperately wanted to go to his mate, but Del wasn't actually in danger. Tyler was trying to protect Matt, not to attack anyone.

"Ryland suggested that maybe Tyler wanted to go with him," Matt said.

He had a hand on Tyler's shoulder. That wasn't what caught Angus's attention, though. No, what did was Tyler in his gargoyle form. It was impossible for him to look away.

Angus suspected most people in the room felt the same way. Tyler was still small, but his muscles looked like they'd doubled in size. His arms, chest, and stomach tightened as he moved and tried to keep Matt in place, his borrowed t-shirt slipping down his front in shreds. His skin had turned gray, and Angus suspected that it would feel hard and cold like stone if he touched it.

Then, there were the wings.

They were massive, and when Matt tried walking around

Tyler, Tyler wrapped one of them around him. He used it to pull him back, but Matt didn't appear angry. Exasperated, yes, but he seemed to understand why Tyler was behaving this way.

He put a hand on Tyler's arm and gently pushed the wing away.

"Ryland wasn't trying to hurt you or me, and he won't take you away if it's not what you want," he promised.

"I just thought that since you said you were Pembroke's best friend, you might want to stay in his room until he comes back," Ryland explained.

Tyler stared at him. His ears had grown, too, and they were now pointed. The hardness and scariness of the gargoyle was an odd contrast with Tyler's tiny figure. In his human form, Tyler wouldn't have scared anyone. The difference between his two forms made him even scarier in his gargoyle form.

"I'm not going to take you away," Ryland continued.

"You bought me," Tyler said.

Even his voice had changed. It was deep and guttural, making Angus shiver.

"I did," Ryland confirmed. "And I'd do it again if it was necessary. I didn't buy you to hurt or use you, though. You reminded me of my brother, and I couldn't leave you there. I'm glad I bought you and brought you here, and I wish you'd believe me when I say I only want what's best for you."

"I don't want to go with you."

It was clear from Tyler's tone that he expected Ryland to protest, maybe because Ryland had bought him. In Tyler's world, it meant Ryland was his master and made every single decision for him.

"Then you don't have to," Ryland said. "I'll be more than happy to help the pack financially support you until you get your feet under you. You're free now, Tyler. The fact that I bought you doesn't mean anything. It's not even legal."

"That's never stopped anyone," Tyler muttered.

"I realize that, and I hate that you had to live through that. You won't ever have to again if I have anything to say about it." He looked at Cam. "Can your pack keep him here? Will it be a problem?"

"Of course not." Cam smiled at Tyler. "Tyler, you're welcome to stay for as long as you want or need. You can even become a Rosewood pack member if it's what you wish."

Tyler frowned. "Is Matt a Rosewood pack member?"

"I am," Matt confirmed. "I haven't been for long, but my son found his mate here, and the entire family moved. It's our home now, and I'm not leaving. You don't have to, either."

That was enough to get Tyler to shift back. His wings vanished, his ears got smaller, and his skin turned pink again.

Then he started crying.

Matt was still by his side and folded him into his arms immediately. Tyler would probably have pushed anyone else away, but not Matt. Instead, he clung to him as if Matt were a lifeline that he needed to survive. Angus suspected that was true, although he didn't fully understand how it had happened or why.

Matt rubbed Tyler's back. "You can even move in with my family and me," he said.

Del squeaked, and Matt looked at him. He raised a brow in question, and Del shook his head, then nodded.

Angus had never had that.

Del and his father could communicate without a word, and it made Angus jealous. He liked that his mate had a loving father, though. Everyone should have one.

"Del's okay with it," Matt continued. "And I can't imagine Cora will have anything to say against it."

Tyler leaned back. His cheeks were wet with tears, and his eyes red. "Who's Cora? Is she your wife?"

"No. She's my daughter. I don't have a wife or anyone else

in my life that way. You'd only be living with me, my son, and my daughter."

Tyler stared at him for a moment before nodding. "I'd like that. I'd like to be part of your family."

"Then, as long as the alpha is okay with it, you will be."

They both looked at Cam, who nodded. He'd been staring at them, but everyone in the room had been. He seemed as curious as Angus to find out what was going on between Matt and Tyler, but he didn't ask.

"I don't see why anyone should have a problem with that," he said. "And, of course, the pack will take care of everything Tyler might need. Matt, you'll take him shopping and buy him whatever he needs to settle in this new life." Cam looked at Tyler. "You don't have to stay in Rosewood if it's not what you want, but if you decide to, I hope the pack will become your home. It's safe for rare shifters and will be safe for you."

"Thank you." Tyler's voice wobbled, and he started crying again.

Matt was there, pulling him close again and murmuring to him.

Cam looked away, possibly to give them privacy, and his gaze stopped on Angus. "What about you?" he asked.

"What about me?"

"Have you decided whether or not you'll stay with us? I don't have a problem with you only visiting, but I'd like to know where you stand. Angela isn't going to be happy if she finds out you're planning on moving here permanently."

Angus didn't know how to answer Cam's question. "Del and I haven't talked about it yet."

"And I'm more than okay giving you more time. What do *you* want to do, though?"

Angus had been thinking about it since he'd met Del, and his answer had never changed. "As long as Del is okay with it, I'd like to become a Rosewood pack member."

Cam's smile could have lit an entire town. "I'm happy to hear that, and I'm sure Del will be, too."

Angus looked at him. Del was hovering by his father, clearly torn between helping Tyler and not wanting to scare him.

He was a good person. He was the best mate Angus could have hoped for, and he was convinced of that even though they barely knew each other. He couldn't wait to see what would happen next between them, but of one thing, he was sure.

Rosewood felt more like his home than Wakefield ever had, and he wasn't giving it up.


"Are you sure this won't be a problem for you?" Matt asked over Tyler's head.

Del saw Tyler stiffen. He no doubt expected to be rejected, and for Matt to choose Del. It would make sense since Del was Matt's son while he and Tyler had just met.

Del might not understand why Tyler had latched onto his father the way he had, but he couldn't deny what was in front of his eyes. Besides, he thought that Tyler and Matt could be good for each other, not just Matt for Tyler.

Doyle had left home, and while Del still lived with his father and his sister, he was twenty and spending more and more time outside the house. He didn't need his father to take care of him the way he had when he was a child, and he'd seen how lost Matt was over that. He still had Cora, who was only six years old, but a huge part of Matt's life had changed after they'd moved, and he wouldn't get it back. He'd always been someone who enjoyed taking care of others, and maybe, taking care of Tyler would help him.

It would certainly help Tyler, who needed someone to take care of him and show him that not everyone was a bad person. Not every human wanted to enslave shifters and use them.

"Why should it be a problem?" Del asked.

"It's always been the four of us. Doyle is gone, but he's not far, and I wasn't sure living with an unknown person would be okay with you."

"It is. Besides, I don't know how long I'll continue living with you and Cora. The home is yours more than it's mine, and I don't think that's going to change."

Matt nodded. "I don't like thinking about you leaving, but I understand it might be time. Have you and Angus talked?"

"Not yet." But they would, and soon. Angus couldn't stay forever without talking to Cam and his alpha. If Angus wanted to stay permanently, then he'd have to move. If he decided he was better off in Wakefield, he'd need to go back.

Del knew which option he hoped his mate would choose, but he couldn't be a hundred percent sure until they talked.

"That man is crazy about you," Matt said.

He was still holding Tyler, who'd finally relaxed. He wasn't crying anymore, but he seemed a bit dazed. It was a good thing that Matt had him.

"I don't know anything about crazy, but I sure hope he likes me."

"You're his mate. There's no way he doesn't like you."

Del snorted. "Way to make me feel like being his mate is the only reason he likes me."

Del's father laughed. "I wouldn't worry too much if I were you. I realize this isn't what you thought would happen when we moved here, but it doesn't mean it's a bad thing. Between your brother dating a pack member and Angus moving here, I feel our family has truly become part of the Rosewood pack."

He wasn't wrong. Del still felt awkward a lot of the time, but Doyle was home here, as was Cora. It didn't matter that it was taking Del a bit longer to wrap his mind around all the changes in his life and feel like Rosewood was home for him, too. He wasn't going anywhere.

He watched as his father gently steered Tyler toward the door. They were softly talking, and while Del was dying to know what they were telling each other, he kept his distance. Tyler had reacted badly when Ryland had tried taking him away from Matt, and there was no way to know if he'd react the same way if Del stepped in. It would take time for Tyler to stop reacting so strongly and to accept he was safe, but Del couldn't wait to see it happen. He felt like it would be good for everyone.

"Del?"

Del turned to see that Angus was standing behind him. He smiled, then frowned when he saw Angus looked worried. "What's wrong?"

"Nothing's wrong, or at least, I don't think so. I just need to ask you something."

"You can ask me anything." Del hoped his mate knew that.

Angus nodded. "I was just talking to Cam about Tyler becoming a pack member, and he asked me if I was planning on doing the same."

Del swallowed. He'd just been thinking they needed to talk about this, but he hadn't expected it to happen now. "Are you?"

Angus's smile was hesitant. "I told him I'd be delighted to become a Rosewood pack member but that I needed to talk to you first. I want to move here, if you're okay with it. If you decide we shouldn't be together, it might be too awkward for both of us to be pack members, especially when I don't need to become one. If you reject me, I'll be safe with the Wakefield pack."

Del frowned. "Why are you talking as if you expect me to reject you?"

"Because I have no idea what to think. I wish we had more time to focus on our relationship and our future, but between the mission and my work, I don't know if we'll have it. That's why I wanted to talk to you today. I'd like to know what's happening between us so I don't have to worry about that, too."

Del grabbed Angus's wrist and dragged him into his arms. He wrapped them around him and kissed the top of his head, inhaling the scent of Angus's shampoo.

Del smelled the same today because he'd showered in Angus's bathroom. He wanted more of that. He wanted more of everything, especially Angus, and the only way to make that happen was for Angus to move. "What will Angela have to say about it?"

"I honestly don't care. This is my life and my future. I'm grateful for everything Angela and the Wakefield pack did, but it's not going to force me to stay with them. I want to be with you. I want to become a Rosewood pack member. This place has felt more like a home than the Wakefield pack ever has, and I don't want to lose that."

"That's good, because I don't want you to lose it, either."

Angus looked up at Del. "Is this you telling me that you want me to move in with the Rosewood pack?"

"It is. I can't wait for you to be a permanent part of the pack." They both would be, and they could take it from there. "Have you talked about specifics with Cam? How you're going to handle Angela and things like that?"

"Cam said that once I decide to move here permanently, he'll make sure I have my own home. There are plenty of empty ones since the pack used to be much bigger, but it'll take a bit of work to turn it into the home I wish for."

"It's good that you're not alone to work on it, then."

Del hoped that eventually, whatever house Angus was given would become their home. It was too soon for him to leave his father behind, especially when he and Angus had only recently met, but knowing that Angus wasn't going anywhere was a relief. Once they were both ready, Del would move in and they'd start their future together.

A lot had changed in Del's life recently, but it was all going in the right direction. He wasn't going to bed hungry anymore, and he didn't need to be terrified of what would happen to his sister if his father couldn't find another job.

The Rosewood pack had saved him and his family, and he'd always be grateful for that. He'd always be even more grateful that they'd given them a home and a place where they felt like they belonged, even though they weren't shifters.

And, above all else, he'd forever be grateful that the Rosewood pack had given him the opportunity to meet Angus.

# CHAPTER SIX

It was time to do the thing Angus dreaded.

He'd been with the Rosewood pack for two weeks now, and Angela was becoming impatient. She kept texting him, asking about updates from the mission and what he was finding out through Colbert's phone. He gave her everything he could, but it wasn't enough. She'd been grumbling that he needed to come home and do his job, even though he was training someone to take his place.

Neither of them had said it out loud yet, but they both knew what was happening. They were both aware of the fact that Angus was moving to Rosewood, even though Angela didn't want to accept it.

She would have to now.

"How nervous are you?" Del asked from the driver's seat of his car.

Angus realized he'd been bouncing his knee and pressed a hand against his knee to stop it. It wouldn't last long, but it was better than making his seat vibrate and showing his mate he wasn't as calm as he wished he were.

"She won't hurt me."

"That sounds like you're trying to convince yourself more than me, babe."

The last word made Angus blink. "Babe?"

"I was trying it out." Del kept his gaze on the road, but Angus saw the wicked smile that curled his lips. "I can find something else if you don't like it. How about sweetheart? Babycakes?"

Angus shuddered in horror. Babe was already pushing it, even though he liked that they were to the point of using pet names. It made him feel special, and he wanted to be special to Del. "Babe is fine."

"I can call you by your name if you're more comfortable with that."

"I don't know what I'm comfortable with. I've never had anyone call me babe, so I guess we should see how I like it and then decide."

Del had successfully distracted Angus, but unfortunately, it hadn't lasted nearly long enough. When Angus looked out the window, he saw how close they were to Wakefield, and his stomach churned with nervousness and maybe a hint of fear.

He and Del were going to Wakefield to talk to Angela and, at the same time, grab Angus's things. He didn't have much, thankfully, so they wouldn't have to come back. By the time he left Wakefield later today, he wouldn't be a Wakefield pack member anymore. He belonged in Rosewood with Del, and while he couldn't wait, the thought of what he was about to do still made him want to puke.

"You're going to be just fine," Del murmured as he reached for Angus's leg.

He squeezed Angus's knee, then let his hand linger there.

Angus wished his mate would never stop touching him. He needed to feel connected to Del, even though he knew he was doing the right thing. Wakefield wasn't for him, and it had never been. He'd always be grateful for what Angela and the pack had done for him, but he also couldn't wait to start his new life in Rosewood. He could have done this without Del, but he was glad his mate wasn't going anywhere. He just had to get over the last hurdle, and he'd be perfectly fine.

The problem was that his last hurdle was Angela-shaped.

"This is Wakefield?" Del asked as he drove into town.

"It is. The pack is just outside, although it's so close that it might as well *be* the town. Most pack members work and live here, anyway."

"It's bigger than Rosewood."

"Well, Wakefield pack has more members."

There was a moment of silence before Del asked, "Do you think Angela would cause a war between our packs to get you back?"

Angus wouldn't deny he'd thought about it, but he doubted she would. "The most important thing in her life has always been the pack. She wouldn't put all of it in danger just for one person, especially not one who wasn't born here."

"She values you."

"She does, and she gave me a job and allowed me to learn many things I wouldn't have learned otherwise. That doesn't mean she can't see that no matter how valuable I am, she can find someone who is even more so. I'm already training someone to replace me, and if they follow what I'm teaching them and keep up to date with the latest technologies, the Wakefield pack will be fine."

"As long as she doesn't try using this against us."

Angus was worried, even though he didn't think Angela would do anything that warranted that. He also felt just a bit guilty. The Wakefield pack had given him a lot and had kept him safe for years, and he was thanking them by leaving. Many pack members would have something to say about that, but that was the thing Angus least cared about.

His mouth went dry when Del drove into pack territory. He noticed a few guards, and he had no doubt Angela would know he was arriving by the time he reached the small building where their offices were located. She'd always refused to have an office in her home, and Angus understood that. He wasn't sure it made sense considering she was always working, but it wasn't his decision to make or to argue.

Sure enough, when Del parked in front of the building after Angus gave him directions, they both noticed Angela standing by the front door. She wore jeans and a sweater and had her arms crossed over her chest. She didn't look angry, exactly, but something was clearly wrong.

And that something was Angus.

He climbed out of the car and hesitated. She had to know why he was here, and he'd half expected her to start yelling at him as soon as he arrived. He was glad she wasn't, but it made him apprehensive.

"I expected you, but I didn't expect your mate," Angela said when they reached her. "I should have, though. It makes sense for both of you to come back."

Angus frowned. "Does it?"

"He's your mate. Where you are, he is. He followed you home."

Angus's stomach sank. Did she really believe that, or was she trying one last time to convince him to stay? "I'm not home," he told her.

"Of course you are, and there's work to do. I want to know everything you found out about the auctions and the entire operation."

She turned around and headed inside the building before Angus could explain why he was there. He and Del looked at each other, and Del shrugged.

Angus wasn't alone. Del would be with him every step of the way, but Angus was the one who had to deal with Angela and tell her what was going on. Del wouldn't do it for him, no matter how much Angus wanted him to. He just wished this entire thing was over already, dammit.

Angus sighed and followed Angela inside. He knew she'd be in her office, so that was where he headed. Sure enough, she was walking around the desk to sit in front of her computer when he stepped into the room.

"I'm not staying," he declared.

Angela stopped moving and stared at him. "You mean you want to go home for a bit?"

She had to know that wasn't what he was saying. "I mean, I'm here to pack my things and permanently move to Rosewood."

The silence in the room was so thick that Angus could almost feel it against his skin.

"You're a Wakefield pack member," Angela eventually said.

"For now, but we both knew I wouldn't stay here forever. I even told you that I wanted this to happen when you agreed to let me stay in Rosewood."

"I remember. I thought you'd see that you could have what you need here. This is your home."

"Not anymore. I already talked to Cam, and he agreed I could become a member of his pack. It's what makes more sense. Del is a member of the Rosewood pack, and his entire family is there. On the other hand, there's nothing keeping me in Wakefield."

"I thought you cared about us."

"I do, but it's time for me to move on. I'll still help Wakefield as much as I can, and I'll make sure anyone who replaces me is trained, but this is it for me."

"Is it only because of Del?"

It was tempting to lie. Angus almost did. "No. I know you did everything you could to make me feel like I was home here, but I always knew I wasn't. Several pack members made sure I couldn't forget."

Angela briefly closed her eyes. "I should have kept a better eye on you."

"You shouldn't have had to. As a pack member, I should have been treated like anyone else, but not everyone did that. I could have come to you, but I didn't want to bother you, and

I still don't. I'm only telling you this because I'm leaving, and I feel you should know."

"Nothing I can say or do will convince you to stay?"

Angus shook his head and reached back. Del linked their fingers together right away, squeezing hard enough to remind Angus he was there. "I'm sorry. I never belonged in Wakefield, and I always knew that, regardless of how welcoming you and the others were. I found my place in Rosewood, and I can't wait to start the new chapter of my life with my mate. I'll always be grateful for what you did for me, Angela, but this is it."

It was where their paths parted, and Angus prayed she wouldn't cling to him in a desperate attempt to change that.

Del couldn't tell how Angela would react to what Angus was saying. He didn't know her, but knowing what he did of alphas, he was aware of the fact that she could create problems for them.

This was something that had to be done, though. Angus would never come back to Wakefield, at least not as a Wakefield pack member. He might visit, although knowing what he did about Angus's time here, Del suspected he wouldn't. He'd found a home in Rosewood, just like Del, and they were ready to start their life together. Hopefully, it would be with Angela's blessing. Del didn't need it, and neither did Angus, but having it would mean the alliance between the Rosewood and Wakefield packs would hold.

Because it wasn't just Del and Angus's future in the balance. Angela could take her revenge on the Rosewood pack, and Del prayed she wouldn't. Angus respected her as a good alpha. She needed to show him that she was now.

She rubbed a hand on her face, suddenly looking tired. "I'm sorry we couldn't give you what you needed."

"You gave me what I needed when I found you. Now, it's time for more, and I found it in Rosewood, and with Del. There's nothing else you could have done. Del is a Rosewood pack member, which means I am, too."

"I wish you'd change your mind."

"I'm sorry, but I won't."

Angela nodded.

Del allowed himself to relax, but not completely. There was still time and opportunity for this situation to become a mess.

"As long as you continue helping us," Angela said.

"I'll make sure the pack is safe before handing everything over."

"That's not what I was talking about. I meant with the rare shifters and the auctions."

"You'll still help with that?"

Angela frowned. "Why shouldn't I? I wasn't doing it for you. I'm doing it because it's the right thing and because rare shifters shouldn't be treated the way you are. Everyone deserves a home, and while you were lucky enough to find two of them, others weren't. I want to give that to them. I want to give them a home and a safe place where they can finally be themselves."

Del hoped she truly felt that way and wasn't just saying it because she wanted her pack to be even more powerful. Even if she did, it was none of his business. He had Angus, and they were going home as soon as possible. It was all Del could care about right now.

"Thank you for everything," Angus said. "We're headed to pick up my things. I'll leave the key in the living room."

"I'm sure I'll find someone who needs a new home."

"I'm glad someone else will have use of it."

Del was relieved when Angus pulled him away. He kept expecting Angela to stop them, and he could feel her watching them, but she stayed silent. They climbed into the car, but this time, Angus was driving. He knew where they were going, while Del had never been here before.

Angus sighed heavily as soon as they were in the car. "That went well, didn't it?" he asked.

"Better than I expected."

Angus nodded as he looked one last time at Angela through the window. "I shouldn't have doubted her."

"You doubted her because you thought she might try to keep you here, and she did." But she'd stopped when she'd realized it would be of no use. That was all that mattered.

"Not as hard as I thought she would. I can't help but feel a bit guilty."

"You have no reasons to feel guilty. You did what you had to do for yourself and me."

Angus grinned. "And I'm happy I did."

Del was happy Angus had, too, especially after Angus parked in front of a tiny home that had seen better days. He'd lived here, and Del almost couldn't believe it.

Cam had given Angus a home, but he'd been honest about it needing to be fixed up. He'd offered to help with the renovations and with anything Angus would need to buy for the house, but Angus had told him he didn't need that. Cam had insisted that since the house was in pack territory and would house a pack member, it was his duty to ensure it was habitable.

Angela clearly didn't think the same way. The house wasn't crumbling yet, but Del wouldn't be surprised if that happened soon. Would it be safe to have someone else live here?

"It's worse from the outside than it is from the inside," Angus murmured.

"I sure hope so," Del told him as they left the car. "How much stuff do you have?"

"Not much. I was only here for a few years."

Del thought of his bedroom back home. "I'd have had time to fill the entire house in two years."

Angus shrugged. "I'm a rare shifter. I've always known that I might have to run at the drop of a hat, so I made sure I didn't own anything I couldn't either take with me or leave behind. It was easier that way."

It might have been, but it broke Del's heart to think that even though Angus had believed he'd been home with the Wakefield pack, he hadn't allowed himself to relax. He'd always thought he'd have to run.

They went inside, and Del looked around, curious. Since Angus had told him he didn't own much, Del wasn't surprised to see that the house was mostly empty. He wandered into the living room, noticing a few books on the coffee table and not much else. He wasn't sure whether or not they were taking the TV, but it was tiny, so even if they were, it wouldn't be a problem.

There were no pictures on the walls, no signs that Angus had a family. He hadn't mentioned anyone, and Del had been afraid to ask. He'd heard stories, especially after moving in with the Rosewood pack, so he was aware of the fact that a lot of rare shifters were alone in the world. It was too dangerous for them to move in groups, and after losing people, most of them tended to be on their own so they wouldn't be hurt by losing someone else.

Hopefully, now that Angus was a Rosewood pack member, he'd be able to make friends and memories. Del desperately wanted that for him and for him to be happy.

Angus had several bags in his closet, and they used that to gather all his belongings. Angus took care of the bedroom while Del focused on the books in the living room and a few knickknacks he found around the house. Angus had told him to leave the kitchen as it was after he'd grabbed his favorite mug, and Del obeyed.

It didn't feel like Angus was leaving much behind, and Del understood better how eager he was to finish moving to Rosewood. He didn't have anything here in Wakefield, but he had his entire future waiting for him in Rosewood.

"We have all of it?" Del asked as he finally closed the trunk of his car. He turned back toward the house as if it would give him an answer.

"We do," Angus told him. "And even if we don't, it's nothing I'll miss, and at the very worst, we can come back."

"The fact that you think that coming back would be the worst outcome tells me a lot about your life in Wakefield," Del pointed out.

Angus wrapped an arm around Del's waist and leaned against his side. "You're not wrong. I'll be happy never to come back."

Del kissed Angus's temple. "Then I'll be happy that you won't, too. Are you ready to go home?"

"More than I'll ever be," Angus confirmed, which was all Del had been waiting for.

He let go of his mate and moved toward the driver's door, freezing when he saw two men coming toward him from the forest. He had no idea who they were, but from their expressions, they weren't friends.

"What's happening here?" one of them asked.

"I'm giving you what you've wanted for so long," Angus said. "I'm leaving."

The second man frowned as he looked from the car to the house, but the first one moved closer to Angus, too close for Del to be comfortable. "What are you talking about?" he asked.

"You always tell me I don't belong, remember? Well, I agree. I *don't* belong in Wakefield, which is why I'm leaving," Angus told him.

"You're abandoning us?" the guy by the car asked.

Angus snorted. "I'm not abandoning anyone. I'm moving."

The man in front of him stepped even closer. "You're betraying our pack," he said with a growl that alarmed Del.

"What do you want from me, Mike?" Angus asked. He stood his ground, not looking one bit scared.

Del was scared enough for both of them.

"You can't leave. You're a member of our pack," Mike snapped.

"Am I? Because you spent two years telling me I never belonged. I finally agree, and now, you have a problem with that?"

"Angela won't allow you to leave."

"Newsflash, asshole. Angela agreed that I could leave. She knows why I'm going, and she has no problem with it."

Mike did, though. He reached for Angus, and Del stepped forward to defend his mate. He doubted he could do much against a shifter, but that wouldn't stop him from trying.

He didn't have to. Angus moved to the side, avoiding Mike's hand and shifting. Del could only watch as Angus's clothes tore around him and fluttered to the ground. His human body was gone, leaving place to a gorgeous white horse.

A horse with wings.


Angus reared back. He'd reached the end of his patience with Mike and Leonard and was ready to pound Mike's face into the ground with his hooves. He didn't care what Angela would think of it. Mike and Leonard were assholes, and she had to know that.

Angus expanded his wings, ready for a fight. Mike snarled and started shifting, too, his nails turning to claws. He could do a lot of damage, but so could Angus. It didn't matter that he wasn't a predator in his shifted form. He was dangerous, and Mike was about to find out how much.

"What's happening here?" a voice snapped from the forest.

All four of them turned to look as Angela came out of the forest. She was naked, a sure sign she'd been in her wolf form until seconds ago, and while Angus, Mike, and Leonard didn't have a problem with that, Del flushed red and looked away. It was endearing, but Angus had other things to focus on right now. He'd have to see if he could replicate the flush on Del's cheeks later when they were alone.

"Well?" Angela asked as she came to a stop in front of them. "Is anyone going to answer?"

"We caught him sneaking away," Mike said.

He was fully human again. He knew better than to show Angela that he'd been about to shift and attack Angus.

Angela frowned. "Sneaking away?"

Mike gestured at the car. "He packed all his things. He's abandoning the pack."

Angela's expression smoothed out. "He's not abandoning us, Mike. He's moving to his new pack."

Mike gaped. "And you're allowing him to?"

Angela narrowed her eyes. "Do you have something to say about my decisions as an alpha?"

"Of course not, but we need him."

Angus finally shifted back. He was safe, and he would be until he and Del managed to leave Wakefield pack territory. Angela had given him her word that she'd let him go, and she kept her promises.

Del was by Angus's side in seconds. He took off his sweater and draped it over Angus's shoulders, for which Angus was grateful. He already regretted shifting because it meant he had one less change of clothes, but he'd needed to be in his Pegasus form to defend himself and Del.

"Let me grab you some clothes from the car," Del murmured.

He was moving before Angus could say thank you. He

grabbed one of the backpacks Angus had filled with his things and came back, wrapping an arm around Angus's shoulders. He started pulling Angus toward the house, but Angus shook his head. He didn't need to be inside to get dressed.

It was going to take a while for Del to learn that. He wasn't used to people going around naked, which was what happened when you lived with a bunch of shifters. Angus wondered for a moment if it was odd, but in any case he'd never understand it.

Angus quickly got dressed, and by the time he was done, Angela was finished tearing Mike and Leonard a new one. They looked like kicked puppies, which shouldn't have made Angus as happy as it did.

"Thank you," he told Angela as he climbed into the passenger seat of Del's car.

She stared at him for a moment before nodding. "I'll see you soon," she promised.

She was probably right. They had work to do and shifters to save, and none of this was going to stop them.

Angus didn't realize he was holding his breath until Del's car reached the edge of the Wakefield pack territory. When it did, he relaxed, and this time, it was for real. His shoulders slumped and he felt like a weight had been lifted off his chest.

He was free, and he was headed home with his mate.

"Can I ask about your shifted form?" Del asked.

"You just have," Angus teased.

Del rolled his eyes. "You know what I mean."

"Ask away."

There wasn't much Angus could tell Del, but he was happy to answer any question his mate might have. It made the drive back to Rosewood pass faster, and Angus was surprised when they saw the first signs that they were headed into town.

With the Wakefield pack problem behind him now, he

could focus on the hurdles still waiting for him. "I'm going to have to spend so much money on furniture and renovations," he said with a groan.

"Didn't Cam offer to pay for part of that?" Del asked.

"He did, but if this is my home, I should be the one paying for it, right?" That was how things had worked in Wakefield.

Del shrugged. "I don't know. I'd never lived with a pack before. Cam seems to take his position very seriously, though. He wants to take care of his people, and now you're one of them. Maybe you should allow him to do that."

Angus couldn't say he'd be sorry. He had some money put away, but he wasn't sure it would be enough for him to do everything he wanted with the house. This was his forever home, though. He could feel it in his bones, and he wanted to make it into the home he and Del would share eventually. He wanted Del to have input on how the house would look and what it would become, even though he'd be the only one living there for now. They hadn't talked about moving in together, and Angus was fine with that. Del was young, still going to college and trying to find his way in life. Angus could give him the time he needed to figure things out.

"I'm going to need groceries, at the very least," Angus said.

"Are you already moving in, then?"

"I think so. I'm grateful for Toby and Cam welcoming me into their home, but I need my own space. I checked the house, and while it's mostly empty, it has running water and electricity. I'm not saying it'll be comfortable, especially until the furniture comes, but I'll make do."

"Why don't we grab some lunch, then? We can get whatever you think you need afterward."

"Let's go eat," Angus said.

He'd expected his mate to take him into Rosewood, but instead, he headed straight for pack territory. Angus didn't understand until Del parked in front of the house he shared with his sister, his father, and now, Tyler. "You meant you were taking me to lunch with your family?" he asked.

"Yeah. Unless you had something else in mind?"

Angus shook his head. He loved the relationship between Del and his family. Matt would be happy to see Del and even Angus.

Angus got out of the car, wrinkling his nose at the two others already parked in front of the house. One car made sense, since Matt needed to get around, but who did the other car belong to? Was someone visiting Tyler? Angus hoped they weren't scaring him. He needed time to get over what had happened to him, and he might never fully get over it. At the very least, he needed rest and not be forced to think about all of that for a few days.

The door opened, and Matt stepped onto the porch. He quickly closed the door behind himself, which made both Angus and Del frown.

"Dad?" Del asked.

Something was wrong. It wasn't only Matt's behavior but also the way he appeared. He was pale, as if he'd seen a ghost, and he kept running his hand through his hair.

"I need you to stay calm," Matt said.

"I don't know if I can promise that. I don't know what's happening."

Matt sucked in a breath. "Your mother is here."

Del froze. Angus knew most of what happened between Matt and Del's mother, so he was aware of the fact that this was a big thing.

"I need you to give her a chance and to listen to her," Matt quickly added.

"Why would I do that?" Del's tone was hard.

"Because she's also Cora's mother, and Cora is only six years old. I can't risk losing her. I can't risk for your mother to get custody of Cora."

Del had no idea what was going on. He'd heard his father's words, and they made sense, but nothing else did. Why was his mother here? He couldn't remember the last time he'd seen her, although he suspected it was six years ago when she'd dropped off Cora and had left again. Del had hoped she'd been there to stay when he'd seen her, but he should have known better, even at fourteen.

And now, she was back.

It didn't make any sense.

"Has she said anything?" he asked.

He wanted to rage, to tell his mother to fuck off and never come back, but he wouldn't risk Cora, and he could see how terrified his father was. She might not be his daughter, but he'd raised her as if she were, and he didn't want to lose her.

Was that something Del's mother might do? Del wouldn't put anything past her, which meant they'd have to be careful.

"She wants to talk to you and Doyle," Matt said. "She, well, she said she wants to fix her relationship with the two of you and Cora."

"Why? She never cared." Del was twenty, and he could count on the fingers of one hand the number of times he'd seen his mother after she'd left home when he was five. Hell, he didn't even need all five fingers.

His father rubbed his face again. "I don't know why she's here. I don't know if she's telling the truth or if she's lying. Either way, it would be easy for her to get Cora. I'm not her father, which means I don't have the same rights as her."

"But you raised her."

"I did, and I adopted her. It doesn't mean your mother wouldn't manage to get her if she tried, though."

And that wasn't something Del could accept.

Del straightened his back and squared his shoulders. "Fine.

I'll talk to her."

A gentle hand touched the small of his back, stopping him from stomping inside the house. "You should probably look less like you're about to take her on in a fight," Angus murmured.

"You don't know what she did to us," Del spat out.

"Not the details, but I know enough. If she's here to fix her relationship with you, you can't look angry when you meet her."

"I don't care what she wants. I just need her to leave us alone."

"Unfortunately, it might not be an option. Let's just see what's going on, all right?"

Del nodded. He'd never been so grateful for Angus's presence. If it weren't for him, he'd have barged into the house and yelled at his mother. He was still tempted to do just that, but he kept Cora in mind as he climbed the porch steps.

"So much for lunch," he murmured. "I'm sorry. You don't have to stay."

"I'm not going anywhere," Angus promised.

Del believed him. Angus was nothing like Del's mother, and he wouldn't abandon him. Hell, he'd had trouble leaving the Wakefield pack, and they weren't even his family.

The house was silent as Del walked inside. It was unusual, and he wondered where his sister was. Maybe with their mother. Del had a hard time believing Pamela was here for him and Doyle, but he could believe she was here for Cora. Cora was only six and cute as a button. If Pamela wanted to be a mother, Cora would be the easiest way for her to make that happen.

"Cora is at a play date," Matt whispered as they walked into the house. "And I asked Tyler to stay in his room."

Del breathed easier. "That's good to know. Are the other child's parents aware they shouldn't bring Cora home?"

"I texted them and Cam to let them know what was going on."

With that out of the way, Del felt more confident as he walked into the living room. He wasn't surprised to find Pamela there rather than in the kitchen. The kitchen in their house was where the family gathered most often, and it would have felt too intimate for Pamela to be there.

She was scrolling on her phone, but she looked up from where she was sitting on the couch when she heard Del. For a moment, there was no recognition in her gaze. She looked almost bored, but then her eyes widened, and she got to her feet as she put her phone away in her handbag.

"Del?" she asked.

Del stopped where he was. He wasn't about to hug her or anything like that. He didn't trust her, and the only thing he wanted from her was for her to leave.

"You've grown so much since the last time I saw you. You had to be ten or eleven."

Del gritted his teeth. "Fourteen. It's when you brought Cora home."

Pamela didn't seem offended. "I'm sorry."

"What are you sorry for?" Del asked as he crossed his arms over his chest.

"Everything. I was never a mother to you and your siblings, and I realize now how wrong it was."

"Is that why you're here? To be a mother?"

"If you'll let me. I want to atone for what I did to you. None of it was right, and I hope that eventually you'll forgive me, but I won't push for you to. I only ask for a chance to make you see that I've changed."

Del didn't believe one word she was saying. He didn't care how eager she appeared. There was no way she was here just because she wanted to be a mother.

She'd had fifteen years to do so. Even when she'd still lived with them, she'd never been a real mother. Del hadn't really missed her after she'd left because she'd always been distant and uncaring, maybe because she'd been so young when she'd had Del and Doyle. Del didn't care why she'd behaved that way. Matt had been young, too, but he'd always been a great father.

Del wanted to tell Pamela to leave and that he never wanted to see her again, but he couldn't forget what his father had said. Would Pamela really try to take Cora away if they didn't go along with what she wanted? Del had no idea. He didn't know his mother. He didn't know why she was here or what she was planning. He just knew there was something more to this than what she was saying and that he probably wouldn't find out unless he acted as if he was giving her a chance.

He sucked in a breath. "I don't know if I can ever forgive you," he said slowly.

"I just need you to try. It's a lot to ask for," she said, her voice soft.

She moved around the coffee table and toward Del as if she was about to hug him. Del's skin crawled at the thought, and he reached back, pulling his mate forward. He wrapped an arm around Angus's waist and held him close, thankful that it meant Pamela couldn't hug him.

She wrinkled her nose. "And who's that?" she asked.

"My mate."

Her eyes widened. "Is that why you moved here? I was surprised when I realized that you and your father left with the pack."

"We live here because it's home."

"Of course." But she seemed perturbed, which in Del's eyes was yet another sign that suggested she was up to something.

"It's nice to meet you," Angus said. "I'm Angus."

"It's very nice to meet you, too. I can't wait to get to know you better. What kind of shifter are you?"

Angus opened his mouth, but Del wouldn't let him explain. He couldn't risk it. "I think you should leave," he told his mother.

Her eyes narrowed. "Your father said I could stay."

"Until you talked to him," Matt said from behind Del. "Doyle already told you he'd meet you in town, and Cora isn't here. She won't be coming back today because she's having a sleepover with a friend."

"I thought I'd see her today. I miss my little girl."

Del almost snorted. She missed the little girl she'd abandoned at only a few weeks old without looking back? At least she'd been smart and had left Cora with Matt.

"That won't be possible, but you can come back. You need to give all of them time to wrap their minds around what's happening. You haven't been in their life in a long time, Pamela. Don't force them into something they're not ready for."

She looked like she wanted to protest, but eventually, she nodded. "I'll be back," she said.

It sounded more like a threat than a promise.

Matt walked her outside. Del stayed where he was, so tense he felt he might break. He listened to the sounds of a door opening and closing, then a car driving off. When his father reappeared, Del stepped away from Angus and grabbed his dad. He pulled him into his arms, hugging him like he hadn't in a long time.

"We'll do everything we can to keep Cora with us," he promised.

His father nodded against his shoulder. "I know."

"I don't know why she's here, but we'll find out and make sure she can't hurt us."

There was no doubt in Del's mind that whatever his mother wanted, it wasn't genuine. The problem was that he didn't know if they could find out what it was without putting Cora in danger.

# CHAPTER SEVEN

Angus scrolled through the data he'd gotten from Colbert's cloned phone, but it was hard to focus on his work and stop obsessing over Del and how he'd taken his mother's arrival.

Angus couldn't even imagine what it would be like to have his mother back. Of course, she hadn't abandoned him the way Pamela had abandoned Doyle, Del, and Cora. Angus's mother had died, and Angus would be overjoyed if he saw her again. Unfortunately for him, that wouldn't happen. Unfortunately for Del, *his* mother was back, and no one knew how to deal with that or why she was actually here.

Angus wasn't sure Del was right about her having a hidden goal, but he also didn't think Doyle was right to give her a chance. Her appearance in their life so suddenly and the way she'd managed to find them even though they'd moved in with the Rosewood pack sent alarms blaring in Angus's mind, and he couldn't ignore them. He didn't want to dismiss that she might actually want a relationship with her family from the get-go, but he also suspected there was much more to this than what she'd said.

Unfortunately, he hadn't been able to find anything when he'd dug into her past. She'd had a gilded life without children, partying, traveling, and getting married several times. If that was what she wanted, then it was good she'd left, because she would have made her children's lives miserable otherwise.

But why was she here if she seemed so happy in the

pictures Angus found? Why did she suddenly want a relationship with her children? That was what he couldn't make sense of, and he was terrified that something bad would happen unless he did.

But something bad would happen if he couldn't make sense of the data on Colbert's phone, too, so after taking a sip of his energy drink, he forced himself to focus on his computer screen again. He was looking over the blueprints of Colbert's home, trying to find an entry point. If they were going to rescue Pembroke and whatever other shifter was stuck there, they needed a bulletproof plan, and that started with Angus.

As he worked, he tapped his fingers on the keys, a plan forming in his mind. With Colbert's phone cloned, Angus had access to the security system that protected the house. He had access to pretty much everything, and luckily for him, that included the passwords.

That meant he could get inside.

He grabbed his phone from the desk and quickly opened the group text where he, Cam, and the others shared information. *Need a meeting ASAP.*

The reactions weren't slow to arrive. *We're available now. Just give us time to get there*, Ryland answered.

*My office is always open. Come whenever you want*, Cam texted back.

So Angus went.

His new office was in his home, and it wasn't much yet. The house wasn't exactly comfortable. It wasn't well insulated, and considering it was winter, it made Angus regret he'd already moved out of Cam and Toby's home. But he liked feeling free and like this was the one place where he truly belonged. No matter how much of a mess the house was, it was his, and that was all he cared about.

Still, he wouldn't have said no to functional heating and a

nice chair for his office.

Del was working in the entrance, sanding the railing of the stairs that led up to the bedrooms. He paused when he saw Angus carrying his messenger bag, then started putting his tools away.

"You don't have to come with me," Angus pointed out.

"Why wouldn't I? You're going to Cam's house, right?"

"How do you know?"

"You're carrying your bag, which means you have your computer. That usually happens when you have meetings."

He already knew Angus so well. "I asked for a meeting. I think we have everything we need to go forward and get into Colbert's house."

Del grimaced. "I definitely need to be there for that."

"I managed just fine before meeting you," Angus pointed out.

"It doesn't mean you have to continue doing so." Del kissed Angus, tenderly at first, then with more force as he pressed him back against the railing.

Angus wrinkled his nose. He liked that Del smelled of wood, but he didn't like the sawdust as much. It made him sneeze, and he stepped away with his nose burning.

"Give me a moment to wash up, and I'll be right with you," Del promised.

Angus nodded and stayed in the entrance while Del disappeared into the downstairs bathroom. They'd decided to completely renovate the upstairs bathrooms, so they'd been using the tiny one downstairs, alternating between staying here and in Del's room at his father's house. It was good enough, at least for now.

Del was back a few minutes later, and they left the house together. Like every house in pack territory, Cam's house was so close that it would only take a couple of minutes to get there by foot.

"Have you heard anything from Pamela?" Angus asked as they walked.

The air in the forest was cool and smelled of damp earth. He'd always loved it, but even more so now that he was home.

Del grunted. "She keeps calling me."

"Have you answered?"

"I don't want to. I don't want to talk to her."

"But you will because of Cora."

"I have to. I can't lose her."

No one wanted to. As soon as Matt had told Cam what was happening, Cam had put things into motion. He'd hired a pack member who worked as an attorney, and together, they were doing their best to make things as secure as they could so that Pamela wouldn't be able to get Cora. The attorney thought Matt had a good chance to keep Del's sister, even though he wasn't related to her. Not only had he raised her as if she were his daughter, but she'd grown up with her brothers, and they were Matt's sons. At worst, both Doyle and Del had agreed that one of them would try to get custody. Still, everyone was on edge, and that included Del and Angus.

"Have you found anything about her?" Del asked.

"Nothing more than I already told you. Maybe Doyle's right, and we should give her a chance."

But Del was already shaking his head. "I don't care what he thinks. He wants to believe she's back and that she truly wants a relationship with us, but that's because he's love-starved."

"He has Marcus," Angus pointed out.

"Yeah, but it's not the same. Marcus is Doyle's mate, not his mother." Del sighed. "Doyle is the one suffering the most over this, and I hate Pamela for doing it to him. I never had much of a relationship with her, but he did."

"I thought she left when you were five."

"She did, but I was always closer to my father. I guess I realized early on that she couldn't give me what I needed, but he could. Doyle kept hoping for more from her, though. It broke him when she left. Now that she's back, he can't see that she has to have a good reason for being here. Besides, how did she find out we were here? Doyle doesn't have social media, and I didn't make it public when I moved."

Angus had been wondering about that, too. "Maybe she hired a PI."

"Could you look into it?"

Marcus had already asked Angus to do so. He was wary of Pamela, too, and he wanted to keep Doyle safe as much as Angus wanted to keep Del safe. "I've already started to. I have to work on it around working on the auctions, though."

"I'd never ask you to drop that to focus on my mother. I just need to know we're doing everything we can to find out what she's up to."

Angus took Del's hand. "We are. I promise."

But they had a lot of work on their hands. Angus was sure that as soon as he told the others what he'd found on Colbert and his home, they'd start planning to get in. It wouldn't take long, maybe a few weeks, and there was no way to know what would happen after they got Pembroke back. Angus suspected Colbert and his friends wouldn't take it lying down.

But that was something they'd have to worry about later. For now, their focus needed to be on getting Pembroke back and finding out why Pamela was here. Angus would make sure his mate was safe, along with his family and the Rosewood pack. He'd finally found his place in the world, and he wasn't putting it in danger for anything or anyone.

# ABOUT THE AUTHOR

Catherine is the creator of several series, most of them paranormal, including the Whitedell Pride Series and the Gillham Pack Series. While she graduated in translation, she decided to go the writer's way because it was more fun to create her own stories and characters.

She's been living in Italy for more than twenty years, but she's a daughter of the North — Belgium to be precise — and she misses it so much that she's already planning to move back.

She loves pizza — probably too much — her son, her pets, and of course, books. She sneaks some reading time into her schedule every time she has five minutes free from writing, demands from her various pets and son, and lastly, housework.

Connect with her:

lievens.catherine@gmail.com
BookBub: https://www.bookbub.com/authors/catherine-lievens
Website: https://authorcatherinelievens.com/
Facebook: https://www.facebook.com/catherine.lievens.9
Facebook Group: https://www.facebook.com/groups/411788002341528/
Twitter: https://twitter.com/authorCLievens
Newsletter: http://eepurl.com/c-uvKn

www.ingramcontent.com/pod-product-compliance
Lightning Source LLC
Chambersburg PA
CBHW060630130626
46555CB00002B/731